CAPTURED

LAUREN BIEL

Library of Congress Cataloging-in-Publication Data

Captured/Lauren Biel 1st ed.

Cover Design: Pretty in Ink Creations

Content Editing: Sugar Free Editing

Interior Design: Sugar Free Editing

For more information on this book and the author, visit: www. LaurenBiel.com

Please visit LaurenBiel.com for a full list of content warnings.

*This is my darkest story, and it is dedicated to the readers who are brave enough to read it **and** enjoy it!*

Prologue

Alexzander

I clutched the box containing a game of checkers to my ten-year-old chest and crept toward my mother's room. It was the game my mother and I played every night, though it was often hard to think about my next move with all the noise coming from the room further down the hall. When the screaming quieted on those nights and The Man yelled for me, my mother would try to shield me with her broken wings.

"Can he finish our game first?" she would ask.

Sometimes it worked, but usually he wanted me to come and take my turn with the women after he and my brother had broken them. When the women had no fight left. My brother was fifteen, and he and my father could handle a fresh one. I was too young.

"Lou," The Man would say to my mother, "you're gonna make that kid more fucked up. He ain't gonna know how to fuck a woman right if we don't teach him."

She didn't argue with him when he said no. She couldn't, even though she wanted to. If she pushed too hard with her voice, he'd push back with his fists. And whatever else lay nearby.

My mother loved me in a way she didn't love anyone else, not even my brother. She hated what he became. He'd followed on The Man's coattails, getting his dick wet any chance he could. The Man wanted my brother to grow up just like him, and he was doing exactly that.

There were no screams that night, though. It was a rare evening when the house was quiet, and I wanted to make the most of it. If we didn't draw any attention to ourselves, my mother and I might be able to play two or three games of checkers before The Man chased me out of her room.

As I eased open the door, the box fell from my hands. The tattered cardboard broke open and spilled black and red across the dirty floor.

The Man stood over my mother as she lay in the bed. "Godamnit," he yelled into her face. He drew his hand back and slapped her cheek.

She lay beneath him, still and silent and very much dead. I shouldn't have known what death looked like at that age, but I'd seen it enough times to recognize it. Her green eyes were pitched back behind her lids. Her usually rosy cheeks had gone white, and her lips had turned a pretty shade of blue. The chain connecting her to the wall circled her thin neck. She'd done it. She'd ended the pitiful life she'd been living since before my brother was born. After nearly two decades on a chain, she'd set herself free.

When my mother died that day, a part of me went with her. The part that still shined with some glimmer of happiness tucked inside that terrible darkness. When she would laugh, loud and full, it made me laugh, too.

Now there was silence. No more laughter from my mother, and nothing to save me from The Man.

CHAPTER ONE
20 YEARS LATER

ALEXZANDER

I exited the diner with my leftovers tucked under my arm and got in the truck. I watched the girl with long, dark hair as she bussed the table where I'd sat. My fingers went for the receipt tucked inside the takeout bag. I liked the way she always signed the slip of paper with a heart dotting the *i* in her name.

Ophelia.

She'd slipped extra ranch into the takeout bag for me too, just like she always did. She knew my order by now: scrambled eggs and ranch. Like everything else in my life, my tastes were fucked up.

I drove home with my belly full and my mind lingering on the normalcy of that damn diner. Today there'd been a man sitting with his family. A wife who wasn't chained up sat beside him. She seemed *happy* to be around him. Behind them sat a trucker who found happiness in the bottom of a pie plate. Normal people doing normal things. Then again, I might have looked pretty normal to them, too.

I shook my head and pulled onto the driveway leading to a run-down farmhouse in the middle of bum-fuck-nowhere—the place I called home. The grass grew tall and free. Wildflowers dotted the greenery with splashes of color. A wooden barn stood tall behind the house, but it was one kick away from falling over. The wood had been cut and hammered into place long before I was born, and it hadn't received any maintenance over the years. And within that barn was a trapdoor that led to a pit of bones.

I carried the food beneath my arm and walked toward the barn. I struggled to pull the heavy door along its worn path in the dirt. It smelled like death the moment I stepped inside, as it should have. Two generations' worth of collected decay lived in that barn. My father's and ours. If I ever had any kids, I hoped the pit would never see a new bone, but I wasn't so sure how realistic that was. Thankfully, neither of us had ever knocked up any of the women we took. I wouldn't have minded the Bruggar lineage ending with us.

I sat down in the dusty wooden chair beside the pit. "There has to be more out there than this, Mama," I whispered, dropping my head back. Her ghost didn't answer, so I responded to the silence. "I know, I know, of course there's not. There's nowhere for someone like me to go."

The Man used to remind us of that. *This* was our world. The extent of it. Our lives started and ended on this godforsaken property. Sure, my brother and I left the farm now and then to steal and sell scrap metal to put food on the table, but we always came home. We wouldn't be accepted anywhere else. Bruggars were cut from a different cloth, The Man told us. The world wasn't strong enough to understand our ways, so The Man made us a world of our own.

I stood and brushed the dirt from my jeans. Claws raked my spine as I looked at the old pig pens, long abandoned. Aged bloodstains colored the cracked concrete. The Man used to love to feed the women to the piggies. He said there was no point in wasting pig food when the animals were so good at cleaning the flesh off the bones. We kept them fed, and they kept the stink down. A symbiotic relationship. I'd learned that term from a science book I found while we were out digging for scrap metal in a landfill. My brother wanted me to burn the book, so I did because I felt bad for him. I'd taught myself to read a little, but he'd gotten all of his learning from The Man. Their lessons centered on how to spread legs instead of books.

I looked down at the pit, where moldy fabric and mottled skin glared back at me. It would have been wise to get more pigs after the last of them died off, but I'd have been the one to take care of them, and I never liked the noisy beasts. I could still hear their squealing in my head at night. They got so bloodthirsty at the sight of a new meal.

But it wasn't just tending to the pigs that soured me on getting more. I also didn't like what we had to do to feed them. With the pigs gone, my brother seemed to let the women hang around a little longer. He wasn't a smart man, but he knew enough to recognize that too many decaying bodies in that pit would draw attention. None of our neighbors lived close enough to ask any questions, but they dropped by occasionally to leave a gift of eggs or an extra pie the missus made. We burned the bodies usually, but that smell still lingered.

And if that smell grew too strong, they'd want to know why.

One time, I'd asked The Man why we had to kill them. I asked why we couldn't keep them around like we had kept Mama. He torched the flesh of my lower back for that, and I never questioned him again. If Mama had still been alive, she'd have told me I was old enough to stop asking and to just do as I was told. To learn to like it because The Man was a whisker away from killing me. Of course, I now knew what was going on back then. Now that I was older and I'd lived it. The Man hadn't been a whisker away from killing me. He'd already done it. I'd been dead inside since the day I drew a breath beneath his shadow. Since the day I was born with the Bruggar name.

OPHELIA

THE SCENT of alcohol was a deity lurking within our old farmhouse. Its pungent aroma surrounded me the moment I entered the house after work. I held my breath and hung my purse on the hook by the door. I slipped off my shoes with a silence I'd mastered. With my teeth clenched together, I reached back to shut the front door. I'd successfully eased it open and entered without a sound, but the rusted hinges gave me away as I closed it.

"Hey! Baby girl, come here!" my father yelled from the living room. His words dripped with the slur of hard liquor. They entered my ears and traveled to my stomach, where they coiled around my gut like a snake, tightening and writhing. "Where's your mother?" he shouted.

My mother had been dead for years. Her cause of death had been natural, and nothing had been out of place when I found her in their bedroom. Well, except for the lack of air in her lungs. She'd looked as haggard as always, but more peaceful than usual. It was a peace that probably came from escaping my father. Whether heaven, hell, or nothingness awaited her after death, it was better than living with him.

Now he was intoxicated enough to forget the absence of the woman who had cooked and cleaned and cared for him for so many years. If he only looked around at the slew of empty bottles and dirty dishes drawing flies on the coffee table, he might have remembered. Maybe he was so drunk that he couldn't see straight.

I froze in the hall as his balding head peeked over the recliner. I pressed my back against the nicotine-yellowed wall and made myself as small as I could. He turned and scanned the entryway, where I'd been just seconds before.

"Where's the girl, Mary Ann?" he shouted.

I shivered and walked the other way until I reached the stairs he'd followed me up so many times before. When he was too drunk to make the climb, when they seemed too monumental to a man so wasted, those stairs protected me. I slipped into my room, the creaky door welcoming me "home." I shrugged out of my diner uniform and hung it on the closet door for the next day. I hated my job, but it served its purpose. It kept me away from the house for a while, and it gave me a chance to save up money. I looked forward to the day I could escape to the city. There was nothing in that farm town for a girl like me. Just a whole lot of farmland and manufacturing plants.

I ran my hand over the comforter on my bed and longed for the days when I had to worry about cleaning the cat fur from my clothes before I left for work. I'd brought home a little orange tabby to keep me company a couple of years ago. It was something to love, something to care for that could care back. On good days, my father would scratch under the cat's chin and rub his ears until he purred. Sometimes he'd even let him have the last bite of his corned beef sandwich. But good days didn't happen very often. The rest of the time, I tried to keep the cat tucked away in my room. Out of sight, out of mind. For a year, it seemed to work, but when I returned home to find the cat curled under my bed with bruised ribs, I knew I couldn't keep him any longer. My father would eventually kill him—he already had plenty of fun slowly killing me—so I drove him to a neighbor's house and begged the farmer's wife to look after him. I hoped he was doing well. Anything was better than living here, though.

I put on my pajamas, sat on the squeaky bed, and stared at the dust-covered television. We hadn't had cable in years, and while the old set had rabbit ears, it wasn't strong enough to pick up any local stations very well, especially since nothing could be considered local to us. So I did what I'd done for all twenty-three years of my life. I existed.

I closed my eyes and thought back on my day. I'd earned some decent tips, most of which I'd stashed in a tin box behind a large stone at the start of our driveway. My father would expect me to hand over some money tomorrow, but I squirreled away what I could. It added up, and it gave me hope. The local regulars weren't phenomenal tippers, but we had a good flow of truckers that stopped into the diner and tipped well. Some probably hoped the monetary nudge would coax me into their trucks, but I wasn't that desperate. Yet.

Only one person hadn't left a tip, but he never paid more than what his bill called for, so I'd gotten used to it. Plus, he gave me something nice to look at. He usually came in with his brother, who *wasn't* nice to look at. His hungry stare gave me the creeps.

The ominous thud of heavy boots sounded on the stairs and derailed my thoughts. I held my breath and hoped I had only imagined it. As I released the air from my lungs, I heard it again, unsteady and sloppy, but clearly there. I pulled the scratchy blanket over my head and closed my eyes, like a small child hiding from the bogeyman.

It wouldn't do any good. Blankets protected children from imaginary monsters, but nothing could protect me from what crept closer to my room.

My door squealed open with a familiar, haunting sound. "When did you get home, angel?" my father slurred.

His heavy footfalls drew closer to the bed. He stumbled near the footboard and nearly collapsed onto the mattress, but he gathered his bearings enough to sit heavily at my feet. The scent of sour alcohol wafted over me like a bad omen. A large, dirty hand fell to the blanket and rested on my thigh. Even through the fabric, his touch burned me. My throat tightened as I choked back tears. I couldn't let him see that I was crying. Things were so much worse when I cried.

"Move over and let your daddy lay with you." His voice was soft and fatherly, in the grossest kind of way. An unnatural way.

He crawled into bed with me, and I fought back the heat of my tears. One fell past the crease of my eyelid and hit the pillow. The sound thundered in my ears, but he was too drunk to hear it. He wrapped his arm around me, and I stayed still as stone for several minutes, anticipating the worst. When drunken snores burbled past his lips, I finally took a deep breath beneath his heavy arm.

Alcohol could be a blessing and a curse.

CHAPTER TWO

ALEXZANDER

The next day, I found myself in the diner again. I sat in my usual booth and swirled the dry, flakey eggs around my plate. Not even ranch could fix them. They'd probably been left on the hot griddle for too long.

The dark-haired waitress came over, her hand on her hip as she looked at my plate. "Those are no good," she said as she scooped the plate into her hand and balanced it on her arm. "Let me have the cook scramble some more for you."

She took the dry eggs away and disappeared into the back, the swinging doors bumping against each other once she'd disappeared. She didn't give me a second glance as she returned to the dining area and bussed the bar countertop. She may not have looked at me, but I had trouble dragging my eyes away from her. Her white skirt climbed up her thighs as she leaned over the counter to get to the back of it. My eyes caught on a purplish bruise, right above her knee. It didn't seem to bother her as she leaned into the barstool to give the counter a final wipe.

A bell aggressively dinged in the back. She cursed under her breath, abandoned the rag on the countertop, and high-tailed it to the kitchen. She returned through the swinging doors before they'd had a chance to close fully, as if the cook tossed the tray into her hands and turned her right around to push her back onto the floor.

"These should be better," she said as she slid the plate in front of me. "Sorry I didn't notice how shitty they were before. I've got a lot on my mind today." The eggs were creamy and smooth, much better than the last plate. She looked around the table and realized she'd forgotten the ranch. "Let me deliver this tray of food, and I'll get you your ranch."

A pang of jealousy crept into my chest as she hurried off to serve another table. On the days when she worked in the diner, I thought of her as my waitress. Mine. I didn't like it when she offered her sweet smiles to others.

After she'd served the other customers, she looked back at me apologetically before hurrying back into the kitchen to get my ranch. She brought out two little cups and set them in front of me. "I'm sorry," she apologized.

"Stop apologizing for shit you can't control, Ophelia."

"Oh . . . you remember my name," she said, caught off guard.

I knew a lot about her, actually. Like the way she tied her dark hair into a ponytail before driving home in her beat-up car. She didn't always drive, though. Sometimes she made the trip on foot and stopped to scratch the head of one of the ponies at the farm on the way to her house. And I knew where she lived, and that her pop's old pickup truck sat out front with nearly deflated tires. I assumed he didn't leave the house much.

I almost met him once, when I was sneaking from her bedroom while she was at work. I had just wanted to know what she was like outside of that diner. How she lived. I was surprised by all the broken alcohol bottles laid out like landmines everywhere. No way someone could walk around this place barefoot. I was even more surprised by the emptiness of her room. It had been void of any life. A set of flower-print pajama pants lay folded on her bed, and I'd picked them up and brought them to my nose, inhaling her scent.

So clean. So untouched.

Her room seemed like she'd never grown up and made it her own, like she was still trapped in her childhood. Even the bedside lamp, with its pale pink shade, looked like it belonged in a child's room. It made me uncomfortable.

Yeah, the girl in front of me right then didn't match the one who slept in that bedroom. I wondered if her soul got zapped the moment she walked into her home, much like mine did. The diner was a breath of life away from the homes that suffocated us in this small, shitty town. I could *almost* forget I was a Bruggar at the diner. Could she forget what waited for her at home?

Ophelia flashed me a white smile. She had one tooth that was the tiniest bit crooked in the front, and it was fucking cute. Her cheeks took on a pink hue as she wrote out my check, and she could probably feel the heat of my stare as I waited for her to hand it to me.

"Have I ever caught your name?" she asked, tucking the pen into her apron. The bell angrily chimed, as if the cook was slamming his hand down over and over. "I'm sorry, I gotta go. See you next time," she said, leaving me awash in silence.

I finished up, grabbed a to-go box off the counter so I didn't have to bug her again, and slapped the money on the table before going to my truck.

I sat in the loud, idling vehicle for several minutes, absorbing a little more of her. She flashed her blue eyes at me through the window and threw me a wave that made me choke on the saliva that had gathered beneath my tongue. I could watch her all day, but I'd end up as big as my brother if I kept going to the diner just to get my fix of her. With a sigh and a final glance toward her, I made the drive home.

Once I got inside, I pulled the takeout box from the bag and put it in the fridge. The old thing barely kept the food cool enough to be considered safe, but we didn't have another option. The handle nearly came off the door when I closed it. Nothing a little duct tape wouldn't fix.

"Alex!" my brother yelled from the basement.

I hate when he calls me that.

My mother named me Alexander, but she never learned to read, so she spelled my name the way it sounded. That was where the "z" came in. Alexzander comes from Greek origin —*defender of the people*—which is ironic, considering what we do. The Man hated my name and said it made me sound like a sissy, so he refused to call me Alex and chose Zander instead. I didn't mind. I didn't like the way my name sounded in his mouth anyway.

My brother's name was Gunnir, which was just fucking awful. Even though there were two correct ways to spell that name, she still managed to fuck it up. I'd take an ironic Greek name over that any day.

We were fucked way beyond our names, though. The Man didn't allow us to attend school. He said anything we needed to learn about this life could be taught by him. I hated being dumb, so I taught myself as much as I could from books. I also learned a surprising amount of random stuff from the women. One had been a psychology student who loved to analyze us. She said we'd been conditioned, that we were kept uneducated because stupid kids grow up to be stupid adults who keep their family secrets by walking in the same footsteps. I wanted to ask her more about that, but The Man had grown tired of her before I had the chance. She'd been right, though. I'd continued in The Man's footsteps long after he was gone, even if I didn't follow his path quite as closely as Gunnir.

A scream crawled up the basement staircase. I knew that sound, and like Pavlov's fucking dogs, I began to salivate. It was the sound of pained desperation, and it went straight to my dick. My body responded on autopilot, working up an excited sweat before I even knew what was happening. The scars on my back tingled—a reminder of all the whippings that trained me to enjoy that sound.

Like a hound on a blood trail, I descended the basement stairs two at a time. When I turned the corner, I saw the source of the melody. My brother's overalls were unclipped and clumped around his ankles. His dark, greasy hair hung like a curtain around his face and concealed his tiny, near-black eyes. A woman was in front of him, bent over the carpenter's table, her chains rattling as he fucked her. Her face was covered in tears, snot, and spit as she fought him until she couldn't anymore. Her eyes met mine, pleading and desperate, but she was barking up the wrong tree. I wasn't much better than Gunnir. The painful erection rubbing against the front of my jeans proved that. Watching my brother fucking that poor girl senseless shouldn't have gotten me hard, but there I was. Hard as fuck.

"I was gonna let you start," Gunnir said through a groan, "but she was looking mighty needy."

With his thick build and towering frame, Gunnir looked like our father. It was as if he'd been copied and pasted into this sick world he'd built. Down to the very shape of his nose, flat and round, he was The Man's spitting image. He even fucked like our father.

"Take your dick out, Alex," Gunnir said as he ripped open the girl's shirt, exposing her heavy breasts.

"No, please," she begged.

The words made me ache. It was impossible to resist that

conditioned response to her pleading. I needed her like I needed water on a warm day. I stepped closer and rubbed her chin, and my fingers slid through tiny rivers of tears and drool.

Her blonde hair hung in tangled strands on either side of her head. Her swollen lips were painted red, and clumps of mascara gripped the lashes around her bright blue eyes. Gunnir loved to hand her makeup and tell her to do it like the day we took her. We picked her up near the college in town, but she wasn't a student. We could tell that from the way she talked and dressed. A whore, maybe. The Man taught us to choose women who wouldn't be missed, and she fit the bill. I didn't like them like that, tired and used up, but she was pretty, and she had one hell of a pair of tits on her.

"Don't you bite me," I told her as I unzipped my jeans.

She shook her head as I pulled out my dick and stroked it in front of her mouth. I grabbed her chin and lifted her face to my cock until I could feel her warm breath rushing over the head. Every shudder of her body against the table made me leak from the tip.

I grabbed her hair and rubbed myself against her lips. "Open up, but don't bite me. So help me god, I'll kill you my damn self if you try anything."

I didn't like to do the killing, so I left that part to Gunnir. He had a taste for it. I only wanted to use the women to fulfill their purpose: my pleasure.

The girl spread her puffy lips for me, and I slipped past them and pushed to the back of her throat. Her teeth scraped my skin. I pulled out and smacked her pale cheek. "No teeth," I snarled.

"I'm sorry," she whispered before opening her mouth for me again.

"She feels so fucking good," Gunnir groaned as he stopped the movement of his hips and basked in her sweet struggle. "You almost wouldn't know she's a whore." He laughed, and the girl squeezed her eyes closed against the word, as if it hurt her more than our dicks combined. "You gonna fuck her when I'm done?" he asked.

I shook my head. I didn't like following on the coattails of him or anyone else. Slipping past someone else's come wasn't what got me off.

I looked down at the girl and pinched her nostrils, cutting off her air. Her cheeks puffed as she struggled to breathe, and her hands flailed at my hips, grabbing me with nails that dug into my pelvis. That was what I needed. The struggle.

I grabbed her by the back of the head with my free hand and fucked her face in a way only a Bruggar man could. Just as her grip loosened and she slipped toward unconsciousness, I filled her throat and let go of her nose.

She took a panting breath as Gunnir pulled out of her. Her struggle had ripped the pleasure from him too. He hated when they gave up halfway through. I'd often seen him shove his dick in a woman's ass to get her squirming again. The pain ripped them from the safe places they crept to in their minds. Coping mechanisms. That was another thing that psych student talked about. They coped with the situation by dissociating and going to whatever happy place resided in their heads. Somewhere outside of the basement in the shit house surrounded by woods in deep east bumblefuck New York.

"Sweet baby Jesus, I come with her like I never did with no one," Gunnir hooted as he shook his overalls and pulled them back into place. "Even when she don't fight, she still grips the hell out of my dick. You sure you don't want a turn?"

I rolled my eyes and tucked my spent cock into my pants. "Not when she's filled with your spunk."

"Mama made you a little bitch, just like The Man said she would." Gunnir laughed and buttoned the left strap of his overalls. He left the right side hanging loose, exposing the dirty t-shirt beneath it. "A pussy is a pussy, whether it's been come in or not." He shrugged and pushed past me, leaving me to deal with the girl.

I wasn't being a bitch about anything. I didn't like the feeling of someone else's come or the way it gathered at the base of my dick, and finding bits of my brother's dried jizz in my pubes wasn't exactly my idea of a good time.

"Please . . ." Her begging broke me from my thoughts.

"Don't. Don't fucking do that with me," I said as I dragged her to her feet and looked at her. I smoothed down her unruly blonde hair. "You're fine. No worse for wear. It's just some dick. Nothing you aren't used to."

Gunnir's come dripped down her pale, dirty thighs and plopped onto the concrete. I curled my lip, pointing to the bucket beneath the spigot jutting from the wall.

"You know what to do," I said. "Go clean yourself up."

She walked to the spigot and turned the handle. Rust-colored water rushed from the faucet and circled a drain in the floor. The metallic scent was almost strong enough to override the tangy aroma of her body odor, but not quite. She gathered the water in the palms of her hands and brought it to her body. Goosebumps rose on her skin from the chill. From the way she furiously scrubbed between her legs, it was clear she didn't have the same affection for Gunnir as he had for her. If she was smart, she'd start pretending.

As I climbed the stairs to the first floor, I dug around in my pocket and pulled out the receipt from the diner. Stuffing it inside my jeans had crumpled the paper, but I could still make out Ophelia's signature across the bottom. Seeing her name tugged at the corners of my mouth. She was a really sweet girl.

When I entered the kitchen, I found Gunnir in front of the open fridge, looking through the mostly empty space for something to eat. "We got any of that stew left?"

I pushed him out of the way and grabbed the metal pot

from the bottom shelf. He'd seen the pot, but he was too fucking lazy to heat it himself. Asking about it was his way of hinting.

I placed the pot on the only stove eye that still worked and turned the heat to high. The bowls we'd need to eat out of were still in the sink from last night, so I washed them and set them on the counter. Gunnir dropped into a chair and scooted toward the kitchen table, helpful as always. He gripped a spoon in his massive fist and tapped it rhythmically against the wood.

When the stew came to a bubble, I filled the bowls and slid his toward him across the table. It rattled along the cracked wood. He stopped banging his spoon like a big goddamn child and started in on the meal: venison stew, the way our mother used to make it. I stared at Gunnir as he ate, shoving spoonful after spoonful into his mouth as if he'd been starved. The big idiot hadn't missed a meal in his whole damn life.

With a roll of my eyes, I sat across from him and started to eat. Gunnir kept talking with his mouth open, gravy spilling from the side of his mouth and flinging off his spoon as he gestured. I shouldn't have judged him—I was born a Bruggar, too—but Jesus fuck.

"I don't get why you don't wanna fuck her," he said through a mouthful.

I shook my head and swallowed what was in my mouth. "It's not that I don't want to fuck her. It's that you've clearly taken a liking to her, and you're like a dog humping a stuffed toy when you like them."

He stared at me, chewing loudly. "What's that gotta do with anything?"

"I don't need to keep explaining this to you. I don't like to follow anyone's dick."

"Why you gotta make it sound like that? Like I *like* following dick? I'm not some . . . some . . ."

I blew out a breath. There were five total brain cells in his head, and they were fighting for air in there. "Jesus, just stop. I'm not calling you nothing. I don't like it. That's it. There's nothing more to it. You and The Man played that way, but I don't."

"Are you calling me an incest?"

I rubbed my temple. "You're as dumb as yesterday's roadkill."

Gunnir stared at me and chewed. "What if we get you one of your own?"

"One of what?"

He smirked. "A girl. Get you a girl." He twirled his spoon. "And you say I'm dumb."

I swallowed. "That's a pretty good idea."

"See, I get them too! It's not just you, mama's boy."

I finished my food. The meat was tough, which was unlike how my mother made it. She did everything perfect. She may not have been able to read a recipe book, but she knew how to whip up a dinner like no one's business.

"So?" Gunnir asked when he'd finished eating. "You ready to do this?"

"Tomorrow." I nodded. "Let's get me a girl."

I knew exactly who I wanted.

CHAPTER THREE

OPHELIA

"I said orders up!" a gruff voice yelled from the kitchen.

"I'm coming!" I called back. I hated when he yelled like that. He reminded me of my dad, the man I wished would die and leave me alone to live in the small house on the hill. Some people hated loneliness, but after a lifetime of angry outbursts that knew no limits, I would have welcomed the silence.

"Thanks," I snapped as I blew a loose strand of dark hair off my forehead.

I balanced the tray on one hand, stacked to the limit with dirty glasses, bowls, and plates. When I entered the muggy kitchen, the cook nearly knocked me over in his haste to shove another tray into my hands. I put the dirty dishes by the sink and took the orders before the cook had a stroke. The smell of eggs and grits drifted toward my nose. It was heavenly. The cook might have been an asshole, but he could make some grits.

I grabbed a plastic cup of ranch and went right back out to

the floor. Table four. They always ordered the same thing every time they came in. Scrambled eggs with a side of ranch for the good-looking one, and grits with extra butter for the big one.

I set the eggs in front of the man with sandy brown hair. He wore a flannel shirt, buttoned up high, but I could still make out the cut of his arms beneath the material. He wasn't overly muscled, but he looked strong. I offered him a grin.

"Thank you, miss," he said with a warm smile.

I slid the grits in front of the man across from him. He was gruff, with a scraggly beard and long, dark hair tied off with a sprig of twine. His filthy overalls hung open on one side, and he smelled like cigarettes and mold. He didn't even offer so much as a nod of his head before he dug into his meal like a ravenous animal.

The other man lifted his fork and looked around the table. I'd forgotten to give him the necessary—and strange—topper. I plucked the two cups from the tray and set them in front of him, fighting back the curl of my lip as he poured the creamy ranch over his eggs.

He glanced up at me with a laugh. "It's good. Don't knock it until you've tried it."

"I'll take your word for it," I said. "Do you need anything else?"

He shook his head and thanked me again.

I went to the register to write out their check, but I couldn't stop my gaze from moving back to him. When he ate, he picked around, careful and almost refined. If it weren't for his dirty jeans and the worn boots on his feet, I'd have mistaken him for a city boy. The man across from him looked —and smelled—like he belonged in a pigpen. They were night and day, those two.

When they were nearly done with their food, I placed the check on the table and started to walk away.

"See you soon," the big one said.

The other man flashed his narrowed gaze at him before meeting mine. I nodded and continued toward the kitchen. The big one had never spoken to me before, but I let the weird interaction drift out of my mind as I went off to clean plates and coffee pots. When I came back out, everyone had left, including the two local men. I went to clean off their table, and while I hadn't expected a tip, I *had* expected payment.

They'd left neither.

"Son of a bitch," I murmured under my breath.

I looked outside and saw the lights of an old pickup illuminating the far side of the parking lot. I marched across the gravel and tapped on the driver's window. The attractive one lowered it, and the low twang of country music spilled from the cab.

"What's the matter?" he asked.

"Y'all didn't pay. If you don't give me what's owed, I have to take it out of my own money," I said with a hand on my hip.

"Gunnir, is that right?" he said, turning to the big man in the passenger seat. "You didn't pay the lady?"

Gunnir shrugged. "Guess I forgot."

I looked around the parking lot. It was empty except for the truck and the cook's little sedan in front of the diner door. I'd chosen to walk to work that afternoon, and now I regretted it. The trees swayed in the breeze, and the cattails brushed against each other, creating a low hum. I took a moment to glance up at the sky—cloudy and heavy without a star in sight. The dim parking lot lights didn't help cut through the darkness, especially since one flickered on its last legs and another had gone out completely.

The driver reached through the window and placed his hand on my arm. The hair on my neck started to prickle, and my stomach knotted on itself, twisting in my belly. If something happened to me out here, no one would hear me scream. The cook was busy cleaning the kitchen, and we were the only people left in the parking lot.

"Don't get your pretty panties in a twist," the driver said. "I can just pay now."

He let go of my arm and I released a silent sigh of relief. I was just being a scaredy cat. He thumbed through an old leather wallet, rifling past wrinkled bills. As he pulled out the bills—all ones, of course—I held my hand toward him. He released them before they reached my palm, letting the night breeze carry them away from me.

Assholes.

"I'm so sorry, miss. Let me help you out," he said as I started chasing the bills.

The truck doors slammed, and boots hit the ground as they approached. I squatted to pick up two singles near the rear tire, but he put his foot on one before I could grasp it. When my eyes rolled up to his, my breath caught in my throat.

"Just didn't want it to blow away. My god, you're jumpy. Relax, Ophelia."

He bent down and pulled the dollar from beneath his boot. As I was about to stand and take the money from his hand, pain seared through the back of my skull and traveled down my neck—a sharp burn before I stopped feeling anything at all.

A THICK BLANKET of disorientation surrounded me like fog. I was draped over a man's shoulder, and pain seared through my head with every movement. I fought the urge to rub at the itchy dried blood on my temple. The man's fingers dug into my thigh and I tried to make a sound, but even my voice seemed lost. I heard a woman say something nearby, but I was too afraid to open my eyes. That would make this nightmare a reality.

"Come here, whore," a deep voice said.

The girl whimpered as a loud rustling sound ended with the clang of metal on concrete. When I lifted my head, I saw the blurry shadow of someone having sex with a girl. A chain tethered her ankle to the wall.

Everything in me told me to struggle, but I couldn't. Even if I could get my body to do what it needed to do, I was bound by the wrists.

Concrete rubbed my elbows as the man holding me placed me on the ground. Another chain rattled, and something wrapped around my ankle.

"Alex, if you don't fuck her, I will pull out of this one and put it right into her," said the gruff voice again. He sounded so far away.

"I don't like it when they're sleeping. What's the point?" the man behind me said.

"The point is busting a nut. Who the fuck cares if they're awake, sleeping, dead, or alive? Shit, pussy like that is good no matter what."

I whimpered and tried to pull forward, away from the prying hands on my thighs, but it was impossible to move. My limbs were too heavy to drag myself anywhere. My skirt rose to my waist, and a low growl came from behind me. Hard hands grasped my hips as they lifted me onto my knees, and the concrete dug into my skin. I felt as if I would fall forward onto my face, but he did everything to keep my ass up for him. The man behind me spit on his hand and rubbed the warm saliva between my legs.

"No," I whispered, but I wasn't sure if it was out loud or in my head.

He didn't respond either way. He pushed inside me, nearly

knocking me onto my stomach. I turned my head to watch the blurry shadow in the corner fucking a girl through horrified screams as the rhythmic thrusts against my ass continued. The shadow wouldn't stop staring at me as he thrust harder, knocking the girl against the table.

I tried to disappear in my mind, but it hurt too much inside there, too. The blow caused a gnawing pain that refused to let up, especially as the man behind me put his weight over me and thrust harder. Every motion vibrated against my tender skull. I moved my arms toward my body, trying to find a way to baby my head.

"Fuck, how does she feel?" the blurry shadow said through a groan.

"She's incredible," the man behind me growled.

"I can't wait to take her for a ride myself," the shadow groaned.

The man behind me scoffed. "No, Gunnir, she's mine."

"We share shit. We always have. That's what brothers do."

I tried to turn over. He wasn't being rough with me, even if he was taking what he wanted by force. He didn't rip through me the way the shadow across the room ripped through the other girl. "Please," I begged, my voice still laced with pain.

"I'm almost done," he whispered as he dug his fingers into my hips.

From somewhere deep inside me, I found my voice. I screamed out.

"Keep fucking screaming," he groaned above me, his hips stalling as he came. "You can scream all you want. In fact, we encourage it."

He turned me onto my back, and the chain jangled against the ground. I was finally able to see him, and another scream ripped through me when recognition washed over me. Through my blurred vision, I could still make out his face.

The "refined" one from the diner. The man who scattered the money across the parking lot. Mister Eggs with Ranch.

I turned my head toward the screaming beside me and realized it was the bigger one forcing another girl. He stared at me as he thrust, going harder once he saw me watching them.

The man above me let his cock rest against the fine, dark hair around my pussy. I flailed, and the more I struggled, the more his cock twitched against me, as if he was holding back from pushing inside me again. His come dripped from me in a thick white trail. My throat burned from screaming. My head was killing me. A sharp ache radiated from the left side of my skull. It was dizzyingly painful, but I knew I needed to fight through it. I kicked at the man sitting on his heels between my legs.

I had no idea where I was, but I could tell it was a basement from the musty scent wafting over me like a thick blanket. The concrete trapped the overwhelming smell of come, urine, and sweat. It reminded me of my dad's bedroom, reeking like the evil that slept within those walls.

I shivered at the thought of my father's heavy steps on the stairs after a night of drinking. I spent evenings silently hoping he wouldn't notice me. I already knew what true evil felt like inside me. Evil that turned from loving me unconditionally, like any father should, to touching me in ways he never should have. Now I'd been transplanted into a new space with the same smells and the same evils.

"Why?" I asked the man between my legs.

He tucked himself into his boxers and zipped his pants. With a sigh, he leaned over me, rubbing between my legs with the fly of his jeans. He pressed his lips close to my ear, and the scent of cheap cigarettes singed my nose. "Because you're mine now, O," he whispered. "Clean yourself up." He motioned toward a spigot against the wall before cutting the tape from my wrists and heading for the stairs.

"Please!" I begged. I didn't want him to leave me down there. I wanted him to let me go. He got what he wanted.

When he made no move to come back for me, I got to my knees, rubbing my head with a trembling hand. The movement sent more come oozing out of me, and the warmth against my thighs made me gag. Maybe cleaning myself up wasn't such a bad idea. I crawled toward the spigot, but the bigger man turned toward me with a harsh glare.

"Not yet!" he yelled out with a powerful thrust that shook the woman in front of him.

I sat back and tried to control my trembling hands enough to pull up my underwear.

Gunnir threw the girl forward, knocking her into the table, and raised the bib of his overalls so he could walk toward me. "Stop trying to pull up your panties, pretty thing," he said as he leaned down. The old denim absorbed his small cock as he squatted on thighs that threatened to rip through his clothes. He reached toward me with a wet hand and touched my face, and I flinched as he grazed my temple. "I had to hit you. I knew you wouldn't come with us on your own."

I tried to tighten my legs and pull my skirt down as far as I could, but it was futile. His eyes locked on the shadow between my legs, where his brother's come still coated me. Gunnir put his big hands between my knees and tore my legs apart. I whimpered as he leaned down until his greasy hair grazed my thighs. He inhaled, then blew out his disgusting, warm breath.

"He don't want me to fuck you," he said as he inhaled deeply again.

I looked up at the ceiling, where the wooden beams crossed above my head. I counted the bands of black rot in each thick shaft of wood and waited for him to do what he was going to do. I closed my eyes as he pushed one of his big fingers inside me with a groan. Tears dripped from the crease of my eyelids as he invaded me with another finger. He groaned, sat up, and dropped his face into the crook of my neck. The stink of sweat and old tobacco hung around him like a putrid cloud.

"Gunnir, come back over here. I want more," the other girl said. The tempting way she spoke caught his interest, and he righted himself and spit chew from his mouth. It splattered beside my hand.

He smirked at me. "Guess we'll have to wait to play," he said as he tapped my cheek with the hand that had been inside me, smearing his brother's come on my face. He went back to the other woman, gripped her hair, and forced her face into the table again.

I breathed a deep sigh of temporary relief as the other victim took the predator from between my legs and welcomed him between hers.

I shimmied toward the spigot, trying to make myself small and quiet as I turned it to little more than a trickle and washed the come from my face and between my legs. I leaned over and rinsed the blood from my temple. Red-tinged water dripped to the concrete and splattered at my feet. I'd probably never feel clean again, but I was as clean as I could get. I slid back to my spot, pulled up my underwear, and sat back against the wall. The rough floor rubbed my bare skin as I brought my knees to my chest and quietly sobbed into them.

Gunnir finished, leaving the other girl a sobbing mess of her own before heading upstairs and leaving us in the dark, damp basement. The girl crawled over to the shared spigot, spreading her legs beneath a heavy stream of water and letting it wash over her.

"Thanks," I whispered. I watched as she tried to soothe the pain between her legs.

"Gunnir is fucking disgusting," she whispered. "And so rough."

I took a deep breath. "What's his brother's name?"

"Gunnir always calls him Alex."

My stomach tightened. "What's your name?"

She laughed. "Just call me 'whore.' That's been my name since I got here."

I shook my head. "How long have you been here?"

"What day is it?"

"September eighth," I said.

The girl let out a weak laugh. "I've been here since April." Her lips tightened. "Time flies when you're having fun, I guess."

My heart sank. Five months of that? How? How could she even take another day of it? We didn't speak as she pulled a pair of dirty pajama pants over her bruised legs.

"I won't call you that," I finally said. "What's your real name?"

She looked at me and smiled. "It's Sam."

"Ophelia," I responded, even though she hadn't asked.

"Welcome to hell, Ophelia."

CHAPTER FOUR

OPHELIA

The chain rattled as I ran it through my hands. The rough, rusted metal slipped across my fingers as I stretched out its length. While the links were light enough to maneuver, they were also incredibly strong. After the men left the basement, I'd spent some time studying the anchor and the cuff around my ankle, but there was no breaking through them. That left me with one option.

Sam lifted her head from the dirty blanket on the concrete floor. "What the hell are you doing?" Her voice was heavy with sleep.

"Trying to see how much chain I have to work with," I said, crawling away from the wall to test the length of the chain. It seemed long enough for what I needed to do.

"For what?"

"I think I can put this around his neck."

Her eyes went wide. "Don't, Ophelia. They'll kill you. Even the nice one will kill you if you try that."

I sat back on my ass. "Am I supposed to just give up? Let myself be one of their sick little playthings?"

Sam shrugged. "If you kill Alex, then what? Ain't no way you're getting that chain around his brother's neck. You'll be dead either way. And then I'll be dead because we'll starve to death down here."

"One of them has to keep a key on them."

Sam dropped her shoulders. "How do you plan to do this?"

I looked at Sam. Months of living in this basement had wasted her away. She wouldn't have the strength to do what needed to be done, even if I thought she'd try. "Do you think you can be a distraction?"

She shook her head. "I don't want to be involved. It is what it is, Ophelia. The quicker you accept it, the better."

I sat up on my knees. "Please, Sam. I have to try."

Sam curled up on her blanket and turned her back to me. "I'll cough. That's it. That's all I'm willing to do. Gunnir will fuck me to death if he thinks I had anything to do with it."

I inhaled a deep breath. "That's all I'll need."

"Your funeral, Ophelia," she said. "But it better not be mine too."

ALEXZANDER

I LAY in bed and thought back on the evening. I'd felt an itch of guilt when I saw her fall forward after Gunnir struck her with the bat. She probably hardly felt a thing at the time, but she was feeling it now. She'd feel plenty now that she was in that house. With us.

Ophelia's body was perfect, and she was such a sweet little

thing too. Always so hospitable at the diner. I felt another twinge of guilt for taking someone like her, but she was everything I needed. She reminded me of my mother, but not in a Freudian way. She was wholesome and kind. It was a blind draw toward familiarity. She felt familiar.

The moment we entered the basement, Gunnir had been on his girl. He'd been hard since he hit Ophelia. I wasn't hard until my hand rode up her warm thigh when I threw her over my shoulder. After that, the anticipation took over, making me ache with a hunger I didn't have before I got my hands on her.

My mind went to the moment I turned her over. Even dazed, she'd recognized me. The dark makeup surrounding her blue eyes had smeared across her pale cheeks, and dark lipstick had painted her lips. She looked fucking delicious. She was better than a steak laid out in front of me. She was like my mother's venison—soft and tender. I wanted to fight the temptation because she was injured, but Gunnir's threat hung above me. He would have pushed into Ophelia if I hadn't taken her, and I couldn't bear the thought of him getting to her first.

I shivered as I thought about my come dripping from her, something I hadn't seen in so long. I'd seen enough of my brother's come to last me the next four lifetimes, but it had been forever since I sank into one of their cunts. I always ended up in their mouths, as far from my brother as I could get.

But this one? She was mine.

Once I was inside her, it was as if she'd been made for me, and I'd have bled Gunnir dry before I let him take her. Anger rose inside me at the thought of it, even long after I left the basement. I wanted him as far away from her as he could get. He had his whore to sink into. He didn't need mine.

I got out of bed and walked into the living room. Gunnir

was sitting on the couch, his fingers beneath his nose. My eyes narrowed as I sat on the chair beside him, and a sly smirk crossed his face.

"What are you smelling?" I asked.

"Your girl on my fingers," Gunnir said with a groan. He was basking in the scent of her *and* me.

"I told you not to touch her," I said as I rose to my feet. "And you're enjoying my come on your fingers, you sick fuck."

"She's not just yours, Alex."

My eyes stayed on him. Gunnir had taken everything from me. Every girl we ever had was his first and mine second, just as our father had done with him. I had to take what I wanted first, enjoy sloppy seconds, or be satisfied with their mouths. I wanted the freedom to go downstairs and fuck my girl's untouched pussy when I felt the ache in my balls.

"Let me have one thing. One fucking thing, Gunnir," I said as he stood to face me.

He towered over me, but I didn't waver.

"You have anything you want. We got that girl for *you*, but she's not just yours to use. Maybe it will teach you that following the dick ain't so bad."

"Fuck you," I snarled. "You're definitely our father's son."

Gunnir laughed. "Sure am. Maybe one day you'll realize that you're his, too. A Bruggar man gets off from the struggle, and you got off from the struggle," he said with a slow lick up his fingers.

"Fucking disgusting. Why don't you just suck my come out of her next time?"

Gunnir's eyes lit up. "Don't give me ideas, Alex."

Gunnir wasn't right in the head. He would absolutely do it, and I had a lapse in sanity when I suggested it. I wasn't right in the head either, but I'd had a chance to care about someone other than myself: my mother. She hadn't made me a pussy, but she'd molded an odd creation that had both the drive to harm and the control to harm less. But I'd never be able to turn off the way I was raised. The heavy hand of The Man reminded my body on a subconscious level that I needed to take what he wanted me to take. I was a fucking Bruggar, after all.

CHAPTER FIVE

ALEXZANDER

I lay awake, frustrated and angry after the conversation with my brother. I kept my door open so I could hear Gunnir's footsteps if he went downstairs. The night had been silent, but I was still frustrated. I couldn't stop thinking about how it felt to get inside her, followed by the intrusive thoughts of Gunnir's dirty fingers.

I was a Bruggar in the sense that I would take that girl as often as I could, whether she wanted it or not, but I didn't like pushing through familial spunk to get to what I wanted. I enjoyed the empty warmth of a pussy. I didn't care if it was too dry because of the disgust for me. The warm, slick wetness of another man's load didn't make it easier to slide into. I wanted to spit on their pussy or in my hand before pushing inside them so that the only thing coating them was more of me. Our father had hated me for refusing to follow them, and my brother didn't understand it. I just wasn't like them in that way.

The Man had also hated how much time I spent with my

mother, who was his captive long before we were born. He'd grown tired of her, but he couldn't bring himself to get rid of her. He'd gotten rid of so many women before her and after her, but something human inside him told him he couldn't kill the mother of his children. But that was the only human thing about him. The Man was a monster, feared by all except Gunnir, who looked up to him as if he were a god. He was no deity. He might have made the sign of the cross over his chest, but it was only to unclip the straps of his overalls.

I was being judgmental. After all, I was just as guilty when it came to using the girls. But I refused to be a clone of The Man. I forged my own way, even if it was still a sin-laced path. I didn't need to break a girl's body to get the pleasure I wanted. Not like Gunnir, who needed to fuck them as hard as he could to pay homage to our father.

Ophelia could hate me all she wanted, but at least she wasn't *his*. I would take her body as often as I wanted, but at least it wouldn't be Gunnir's dick pressing between her legs.

I heard what sounded like footsteps in the kitchen. My ears perked and my back straightened.

Gunnir better not be trying to sneak downstairs.

Ophelia was mine. He *knew* she was mine, and no one would put a hand on her but me. The thought of him touching her again lit the anger inside me.

I put on a pair of sweatpants and made my way to the basement. I flipped on the light and both girls stirred. The whore's attention shot to me, but she threw her blanket over her head to shield her eyes from the light when she realized I wasn't Gunnir. Ophelia didn't lift her head from her curled position on the floor. Brown stains painted her white diner uniform, even after only a few hours in the basement.

I walked over and squatted beside her, behind the curve of her back. Her dark hair fell across her cheek, and I wanted to move it. I wanted to see her face again. Her thick lashes and full lips called to me.

The whore coughed and when I looked back at her, Ophelia sprang up.

Something cold and hard pressed against my neck. My fingers flew to the source, and I realized it was the chain. She really hadn't thought this through. While one end attached to the anchor, the other was through the cuff around her ankle. I reached down and gripped the chain, yanking until she lost her balance. Unfortunately, *I* hadn't thought that through, and now her full weight hung from the chain around my neck.

"Fuck you," I said through clenched teeth.

I threw my weight backward, knocking her against the wall. The air left her lungs, and she lost her grip on the chain. I turned and pinned it against her neck. Her hands clawed at the metal, fighting to free enough space to draw a breath.

I leaned closer to her face. "I was coming down here to make sure my fucking brother wasn't going to touch you, and you pull *this* shit?"

Her face reddened, her cheeks puffing to try to pull air she wouldn't find.

"If you try something this fucking dumb again, I will kill you. Do you understand? You're mine. Mine to own. Mine to use. Mine to discard if you can't act right. I was trying to look out for you, O." I replaced the chain with a firm grasp on her throat as I reached down with my other hand and pulled out my cock. "I wasn't going to fuck you again tonight, but you need to learn from this mistake." I raised her skirt and gripped her ass. My eyes bore into hers.

Please, she mouthed, tears dripping onto my wrist.

I spit on my hand, and the moment I touched between her legs, her eyes rose to the ceiling and her hands stopped pushing against me. I lifted her thigh with a warm, wet hand and pushed inside her. A small noise left her mouth, but her eyes remained locked above us.

"Look at me," I commanded, but not even an angry thrust of my hips drew her attention to me. She'd traveled somewhere else in her mind.

I dug my fingers into her thigh, and she cried out as I drove my hips further into her. She could travel somewhere else in her mind, but her body was still here.

My toy.

Mine.

I bottomed out inside her, with an inch of my dick to go. I pushed my hips deeper, forcing that final bit of me into her until I felt her soft hairs against mine. She puffed her cheeks and pursed her lips as she fought the pain. Her nails dug into my wrist, the smallest sign of fight she gave me. I hated that she didn't fight me and that her tears silently fell. Even as her fingers dug into me, she refused to acknowledge what was happening to her. It had taken the whore a long time to stop fighting, but Ophelia seemed broken before my dick ever touched her.

I leaned over and bit her shoulder hard enough to make her body jolt, and yet her eyes remained on the ceiling. I pulled my hand away and brushed the dark hair off her sweaty forehead. "You're mine, O. You might as well get used to it."

"No," she whispered. She dropped her head back, the only sign of her returning to this room with me.

"Yes. And if you ever pull shit like that again"—I gestured to the chain—"instead of fucking you, I'll kill you." When she didn't respond, I smacked her. Her cheek reddened beneath the blow. "Do you understand?"

She nodded.

I pulled out of her and released her thigh. She continued to avoid my gaze, choosing to watch as my come slid down her legs instead. I reached between her thighs and gathered as much of my come as I could. I turned toward the whore, ripped the sheet off her, and lifted her by her hair before shoving my coated fingers into her mouth. I held her nose until her body lurched with desperation. When she panted for air, I spit in her mouth. "Don't be a dick. She wouldn't have gotten fucked tonight if you didn't try to help her," I snarled as I spit again, soaking her chin as she tried to recoil. I released her hair, and she gagged and heaved on all fours.

Ophelia sobbed silently against the wall, and I felt a moment of guilt before anger surpassed it. I really wasn't going to fuck her, but then she'd tried to kill me.

Chapter Six

Ophelia

I dragged the chain along the floor, letting it catch in every blemish it found. The rattle echoed off the walls. If I kept busy with such an idle task, I wouldn't think about the raw places on my ass from Alex pressing me against the rough walls. I'd done something stupid, and the ache between my legs reminded me of that. I should have listened to Sam. I was so blinded by the prospect of freedom, I hadn't thought things through. Killing Alex meant being left to his brother, which was worse. Much worse. Even in his anger, with his face twisted with rage, Alex didn't go out of his way to hurt me. He fucked me harder, sure, but he could have done so much worse.

Footsteps rattled the stairs, sending plumes of dust scattering outward. That heavy gait didn't belong to Alex, and I found myself instinctively wishing for him instead. Gunnir was fucking disgusting—a hideous man with a primitive mind.

"Heard you were a bad girl, whore," Gunnir cooed as he squatted beside Sam. She rolled her eyes up his body.

"I didn't—"

Gunnir slapped her across the face, knocking her backward. "Don't lie to me. I know what you did."

Sam leaned over and babied her cheek.

"Y'all ain't good for each other," Gunnir snarled. "She's making you brave, and you best think better of it because I've killed women for less than what you two did last night." Gunnir laughed. "The best part? Y'all attacked the good one. The mama's boy. Little pussy of a man."

"Why's he a pussy?" Sam asked, her chin rising in defiance. "Because he doesn't like sloppy seconds?"

"Am I in the looney house? Why do you people think it's about who came first?" Gunnir shook his head.

What was she doing? Why was she pushing him? I didn't know them as well as she did, but I knew enough to know there were layers of fucked-up between Gunnir and Alex. I had no idea what the layers held, and to be honest, I was afraid to find out.

I tugged my knees toward me, holding the chain against the ground to keep it quiet, trying to make myself as small and silent as possible. I didn't want Gunnir to notice me. I didn't even want him to remember I existed.

"I know what you're doing. You're trying to get in my head and shake everything up in there." Gunnir grabbed Sam by the hair and dragged her to the table. My breath hitched. I didn't want to see or hear him force her again, but I was more horrified by what he did instead. He grabbed a hammer and twirled it around as he took Sam's hand and held it on the table. "My brother is a bitch. But we're family." Gunnir laid his weight on her hand as she threw herself backward.

"You can fuck me any way you want, Gunnir, just don't do that," she pleaded.

Gunnir's gaze snapped to her face. "I can fuck you however I want anyway. I don't need your permission. What the fuck kind of bribe is that? You wanna offer something, it better be something I haven't gotten yet."

Sam looked back at me, and I couldn't take a breath. The air was trapped in my lungs. I was scared she'd offer Gunnir the one thing he hadn't gotten: me.

But she didn't. She dropped her shoulders and looked away from me. "Get it over with," she said.

Gunnir leaned over her, raised the hammer, and brought it down with a nauseating crack. I held my ears to drown out Sam's screams, but the desperate sounds found their way through the barrier and into my brain. Gunnir raised the hammer and brought it down again.

Steps thundered across the floor and my eyes flew open, afraid I'd find Gunnir barreling toward me. I looked up and saw Alex yanking his brother backward. Sam ripped her arm away, clutching two crooked, discolored fingers with her other hand. I lowered my hands as Gunnir gestured toward me.

"Your turn," he said, turning his massive body toward me.

Alex stepped between us. "No."

"What do you mean? My girl isn't the only one who's gonna get punished for that stunt." Gunnir jabbed his finger in my direction. "She's the one that tried to kill you!"

Alex stood taller. "She got her punishment last night."

"What, did you fuck her all sweet and gentle like?" Gunnir walked toward me and lifted me to my feet by my arm. I squealed as he ran a dirty hand up my thigh. He turned me around and pushed my chest against the wall. "Do I need to show her what a real punishment is? Maybe fuck her ass?"

The concrete grated against my cheek, and I cried as his hands moved beneath my skirt and grabbed my ass. His fingers passed over the sore places from Alex last night. Tears slipped down my cheeks in heavy drops that hit my chest.

"Oh, sweet mama's boy fucked you real good last night, huh?" Gunnir groaned in my ear. His breath was hot and tangy, like he'd been eating barbecue.

"Leave her alone," Alex said with a sharp rise in his tone. It wasn't out of benevolence, though. It was out of possession, like Gunnir had grabbed a toy he wasn't finished playing with.

"How's your little cunt feel? Sore?" he asked as he groped between my legs, and I flinched as he pushed his fingers inside me. My body went rigid, and the pain between my legs radiated up my spine.

"I said stop, Gunnir. Enough!" Alex gripped his brother's shoulders and yanked him away from me.

Gunnir raised his wet fingers and licked them as he backed away. "Fuck, Alex. I don't eat pussy, but with her, I just might. So sweet and clean."

Oh god, no. I couldn't deal with his mouth on any part of me. Neither of them. They were both sick fucks.

"Fuck off!" Alex yelled. He squared off against his brother.

Gunnir raised his shirtsleeves, readying to fight, and Alex didn't stand down. He started to unbutton his flannel shirt, exposing a white undershirt. Before anyone could throw a punch, the sound of the doorbell drew their attention.

"Probably the damn neighbors with some more eggs and milk," Gunnir said with a growl. "Keep these bitches fucking quiet."

"That would have been a lot fucking easier if you hadn't broken the whore's goddamn fingers," Alex snapped.

Gunnir stopped and turned back toward Alex with fire in his eyes before climbing the stairs. The basement door slammed, and Alex turned toward us. Sam cradled her hand to her chest in the corner. I stayed against the wall, my back pressed into the concrete.

"Both of you better stay fucking quiet. If you make a

sound, I'll get the shotgun and blow your brains out before the police can get here."

"Alex . . ." I whispered. "You could let us go. You have the keys, don't you?"

Alex's eyes narrowed. "I think you've gotten the wrong idea. I might be less shitty than Gunnir, but I am not kind." He stepped closer and fisted my hair, sending a whimper up my throat. "I don't want to save you. The moment I fucked you, you became mine. I own you. Your body is mine to use whenever and however I want. Why the hell would I want to let you go? I'm nowhere near done with you."

His words were like a knife to my stomach. I closed my eyes as his hand fell to my throat, expecting him to force me again.

The basement door whipped open. "Alexzander!" Gunnir yelled from upstairs.

Alex took a deep breath. "Your mouth and pussy are safe for now, O, but I'll be back for you."

ALEXZANDER

I CLOSED the basement door behind me and saw Gunnir trying to balance the cartons of eggs and glass bottles of milk. I ran over and lightened his load, scooping some cartons beneath my arm and taking one of the half-gallon bottles. We carried them to the fridge, and I kicked the door open with my foot so we could put them all inside. The neighbors were kind, always stopping by to give us fresh eggs and raw milk, and they never stuck around or waited to be invited inside, which was good since we didn't allow visitors here.

"You look fucking weak when you do that, you know?"

Gunnir put the last bottle in, and the glass clinked together as he closed the door.

I cocked my head at him. "What?"

"You let them get away with trying to kill you."

I scoffed. "She wasn't going to kill me. It was just a half-hearted attempt at freedom. They all try to make a great escape at least once."

Gunnir narrowed his eyes. "I didn't break my girl's fingers over no half-hearted attempt for your girl to just get some dick."

I raised my gaze to meet his. "I guarantee Ophelia would rather have her fingers broken than be fucked by me."

Gunnir laughed. "Fair point. I think they're bad for each other, though. Down there, all planting."

Planning, not planting. But now wasn't the time to correct him. "What the hell would you suggest? Kill yours or mine?"

"We could get rid of mine," Gunnir said with a shrug.

"Do what you want, but I'm not sharing Ophelia like we shared the whore. Unless you want to start jerking off into an old sock, I suggest you keep her alive."

Gunnir released a full-bellied laugh that echoed in the small kitchen. "Start? I ain't ever stopped jerking off into a sock."

I thought for a moment. "We could chain Ophelia in my room. Then they won't be 'planting' nothing," I mocked.

Gunnir shook his head. "No. You just want to keep her locked away from me. I like to watch her when I fuck mine. Pretty thing she is. Makes me come harder."

For being as dumb as he was, he'd figured out my ulterior motive. That was precisely what I wanted to do. It was selfish and not very Bruggar-like to want to keep her for myself, but I didn't care. I'd spent my whole life watching Gunnir get everything and anyone he'd ever wanted. It was my turn to have something to own.

"Fine," I said through clenched teeth. I had a plan, and if it had any chance of working, Gunnir needed to think it was his idea.

I went to my room and eyed the closet. The door was falling off the hinges, and some of the wooden slats were missing. I needed to repair it soon. I kept some of my mother's things in there, and if Gunnir found them, he'd burn them in front of me. I touched the box that held papers from when she and I had learned to write with the help of a book from the library. Gunnir still didn't know how to write *or* read, and the latter was why he couldn't drive. If he were by himself, he'd be halfway to Mexico before he realized he'd been going the wrong way. As much as he hated my literacy, I knew he was glad I could read road signs. It made it easier to find women outside of a one-mile radius. If we hunted too close to home, we were more likely to get caught. The Man always used to tell us that, at least.

The box also held the clip that had pulled my mother's thin hair away from her face and a bead bracelet I made for her. I'd taken both things from her body before The Man threw her in the bone pit with the others. Gunnir would destroy them all because they were tangible things that told him what our mother and I had was real. That he'd never had any of that with her, even though he didn't want it.

The wrong parent died that day. I'd remedied that injustice later, but I wished I'd had the strength to do it sooner. It would have saved my mother and so many other women. But it was what it was, and we were who we were.

I looked at the bedside table rotting against the wall. I pulled it away until I could see the metal plate screwed firmly into the hardwood, a chain loop rusting on top of it. A tide of memories rushed toward me. When I was younger, I'd been kept chained too—my punishment for rebelling against the system The Man created. I had tried to get my mother off the chain, and he couldn't allow that. He tethered me to my bedroom until I learned that freedom for me meant captivity for others. There was no way around it. I had to learn the system or become the waste rotting beneath the barn floor.

Now I wanted to attach Ophelia to this chain. Make her sleep in bed with me. Fuck her with the old mattress beneath her to cushion each thrust. Maybe she'd even find some comfort in my presence the way I found comfort in my mother's presence. Maybe she'd fall for me. But even if she did, it wouldn't matter. Love had never been enough within these walls.

CHAPTER SEVEN

OPHELIA

The rhythmic notes of clanking metal—the sound I focused on when Alex used me. I tuned out the groans and grunts from Gunnir as he fucked Sam, and I somehow blocked out Sam's whimpers and the rock of the table as the wheels creaked back and forth on the divots in the floor. I focused on the melody of our chains instead. My chains sang with a soft sound as Alex nudged my body forward. Sam's tune was violent and off rhythm, like a song with missing notes.

I kept my head turned away from Alex as his warm breath washed over me. I couldn't look to the side because I'd see Gunnir staring, digging his fingers into Sam's ass as he licked his lips and glared at me with glazed eyes. If I looked up, I would get glimpses of the man over me. There was nowhere to look that allowed me to disappear in my head except for the rusted hook hanging from a nail with a dusty whip clinging to it. The dark splotches on it were surely from old blood.

"Look at me," Alex growled above me.

"No," I said with a shake of my head. "You get my body, but not my mind." I kept my voice low so Gunnir wouldn't hear me.

His thrusts grew harder, shaking me from the hiding place in my mind. My reality rushed toward me in a nauseating tsunami of sounds and smells. I blinked heavily, trying to fight against the current and slip into my safe space again, but I experienced all of it. The rub of the concrete against my ass. The way he stretched me and spread my thighs. His hands on my chest beneath the unfastened buttons of my uniform. The smell of urine and body odor from Gunnir, and the noxious scent of his come, which I could nearly taste. It was the most overpowering of all, probably because I feared it the most. The scent of bar soap wafted over me from above. Alex was a piece of shit, but at least he wasn't Gunnir. At least he was fucking clean. I was glad I had Alex if I was forced to choose one, but I wanted neither.

I hated him. I hated them.

Focus on the rattle of the chain, I reminded myself as Alex's hand raced down my side and gripped my ass. He leaned into me, and I closed my eyes.

"Do you want out of this basement, O?" he whispered in my ear. I didn't know what he meant, but I whimpered out a yes before he could explain. I knew he didn't mean an escape. He could have meant death for all I knew, yet I nodded. "Be a good girl for me."

I'd been nothing but good for him. I stopped fighting him, even when he took me twice in the past day. I hadn't tried to kill him again. I was being as good as I could be.

The scent of body odor drifted closer, and my stomach twisted as heavy footsteps approached my head. Gunnir's hand rested on his hip, holding his pants up, his dick exposed but spent. He squatted down and brushed my hair from my cheek. His cock was too close to my face, a bead of come perched on the puffy head. His stare was somehow more invasive than what Alex was doing between my legs.

"I want her to suck my dick," Gunnir said with a gap-toothed smile. He brushed his hand over my cheek, and my eyes rushed to Alex.

Alex shook his head and ignored him.

"Oh, don't be like that, Alex," Gunnir said.

Alex put his mouth on me in a show of possession, capturing my lips with his and kissing me hard. His hand wrapped around the back of my neck and pulled me deeper into him. A growl left Gunnir's throat. I wanted to rip away from Alex's kiss, but I knew what would be put in my mouth instead. I'd take his tongue over Gunnir's dick any day.

When Gunnir didn't leave, Alex released my mouth, pulled out of me, turned me onto my stomach, and dragged me toward him. He fisted my hair and forced my cheek onto the dusty concrete. When I exhaled, it blew up the dirt that had gathered on the floor. He leaned over me and pushed himself inside me, covering me with his body.

I knew why Alex did what he did. It wasn't to save me from his brother. It was to keep me for himself. Either way, I'd take it.

"Fuck off, I'm not done with her," Alex growled.

"I don't like that you don't share her," Gunnir snarled.

"And I don't like that you fucking reek. Go clean yourself up."

Gunnir mumbled a battalion of fuck-laced curses before I felt him stand up and back away. The hair on the back of my neck relaxed.

Alex leaned toward my ear. "I need you to do something incredibly fucking stupid," he whispered.

I didn't respond. I couldn't.

"Try to kill me again."

I whimpered, but it wasn't from his weight bearing down on me. It was from shock.

"Alex!" Gunnir yelled from upstairs.

His warm breath rushed against my ear as he exhaled his frustration. "Forget what I said for now. Tell no one."

I nodded as he groaned and came inside me, but how could I just forget what he said? I had so many questions. And of course I wouldn't tell anyone, especially Sam. My stupidity had landed her with broken fingers. I wouldn't put her through that—or worse—again.

Alex pulled out of me and said nothing more. He got up and climbed the stairs as if the strange conversation hadn't passed between us. I rolled onto my back and panted as my chest was finally allowed to expand once more.

Sam scoffed. "I'm so jealous that you have that one. He may be rapey as fuck, but at least he seems like he has half a heart in his chest." A pained laugh crossed between us as she washed herself up. "I saw that kiss," she said.

"He only did it to keep Gunnir's dick out of my mouth," I said as I joined her at the spigot.

Sam shrugged. "Shit, that's sweet."

My eyes leapt to hers. "Your bar is fucking low."

"Get fucked by Gunnir for months and see how low your bar drops."

"I don't know how you do it," I said.

"What choice do I have?"

I sighed, because she was right. We were fully at their mercy.

ALEXZANDER

I THOUGHT I would've had a few more minutes inside her to formulate the idea kicking around in my mind. Gunnir hadn't helped the situation. I couldn't think about a plan when I was trying to keep his dick out of her mouth. She hadn't even had *me* inside her mouth yet. She was mine and he kept creeping too fucking close to what belonged to me. Had I tried to fuck Sam since Ophelia got here? Not once.

He had his. I had mine.

The stress of the situation had set me on edge. I needed something to soothe my nerves, so I went to my bedroom closet and pulled the box of checkers from its hiding place beneath an old blanket. I missed playing this simple game with my mother. She used to beam with pride when I made a smart move. I missed that too.

Had I made a smart move with Ophelia, or had I backed myself into a corner?

I needed to get her out of the basement before he got to her any more than he already had. His fingers had been inside her, and he'd tasted her cunt. He'd had too much of her already. I had to be careful, though. If he thought I was "planting" something, he'd flip, just like The Man had when he found out I tried to get my mother off the chain. He hadn't just chained me to the floor after that. He'd also taken out his white-hot rage on the girl he'd been fucking at the time. He'd torched her and nearly lit our whole house on fire. I tasted burning flesh with every breath for weeks after that, and she hadn't done a thing to him. She'd just been in arm's reach when *I* pissed him off.

If Gunnir thought I was plotting against him, he'd do something much worse than set Ophelia on fire. I considered him a carbon copy of the man, sure, but he was that and then some. He was worse.

Involving Ophelia might have been a huge mistake, but I'd know soon enough if she spilled what I told her to Sam. The whore had a big mouth. They both might.

Chapter Eight

Ophelia

S am and I slept, woke, and slept again. There wasn't much
else to do in the basement. Time didn't exist. There were
no windows to let in sunlight or give us a glimpse of a starry
sky. The best gauge seemed to be mealtimes, but my stomach
said we were often forgotten. We didn't talk much. I think we
were too afraid our voices would carry up the stairs and draw
unwanted attention.

As we sat in silence, we heard the men yelling about
something upstairs. We couldn't make out the words, but the
tone of the discussion was undeniable. Whatever they were
talking about had pissed them off.

When Gunnir's steps thundered down the stairs, Sam sat
up on her knees. I shrank as much as I could and scooted into
the shadows. I didn't want him to notice me. I prayed he
wouldn't.

"Alex is such a little bitch!" Gunnir yelled, and his voice
crawled toward me until there was no way to avoid it. Sam and
I kept quiet as he stampeded around the room. My heart

raced, thundering louder than his footsteps. "He's being shellfish!"

Selfish? I thought, but I didn't dare correct him.

"Selfish?" Sam said, interrupting his pacing.

Fuck.

"Yeah, that's what I fucking said," he snarled. "He doesn't want to share. But that's what we do. We share."

"She's his new toy, Gunnir. Just leave him be. He'll get bored once she's not so shiny and new."

My eyes leapt to Sam. I wasn't sure if she realized the idea she was passing to someone like him.

"You're right, whore. She's too new." He ran his massive hand through his hair, his fingers entangling in the mess of knots. He stepped toward me, and I smelled him before he got to me. His hand found my hair and pulled me to my knees by my scalp. "You need to be less shiny, don't you?"

I shook my head, whimpering in his grasp. Before I could release a scream and call for Alex, Gunnir's dirty hand flew over my mouth. It wasn't that I wanted Alex, but he would at least save me from his disgusting brother. Gunnir was a fate worse than death.

"Shhh, sweet thing," he cooed in my ear.

His body pressed against me, and my stomach clenched and twisted in my belly. He laughed low in his chest as he unbuckled one of the straps of his overalls. I shook my head beneath his hand, trying to pull away enough to scream, but his hold refused to weaken. Gunnir's overalls fell to the floor, and his free hand raced toward my ass and pushed me against the wall. He prodded between my legs with his stubby dick then spit into his hand.

I had to stop him. Even if I managed to scream, Alex wouldn't make it down the stairs before Gunnir forced himself inside me. Pulling my tongue back as far as I could to avoid tasting his skin, I opened my mouth. His flesh pressed between my teeth, and I bit down until I tasted blood. He yelled out and took a step back.

"Fucking bitch!" he screamed. He gripped my shoulder and whipped me around. In one swift motion, he brought back his arm and sent his fist into my face. I screamed out and fell to the ground in a panting mess of tears.

Footsteps pounded on the stairs once more, and I looked up to see Alex. He took in the scene. Gunnir's pants were still down. My skirt was still lifted. His brother cupped his hand against his chest, and my nose poured blood onto my outfit.

"What the fuck, Gunnir?"

"I just wanted to make her less fucking new," he said as he shook out his hand.

"What does that even mean?"

"I thought if I broke her in a little, you'd be more willing to share."

Alex turned toward me, walked over, and lifted my chin. "You might have broken her nose, you fucking brute."

"She deserved it." Gunnir spit at the ground in front of me and tried to tug up his overalls without using his injured hand. "I'm not done with you, shiny little thing," he said toward me. He went upstairs, clutching his wounded hand to his chest as if it were a baby bird.

Alex lifted me to my feet and lowered the hem of my skirt. Blood stained my chin, my chest, and the entire front of my dress. "Let's clean you up," he said as he dragged me to the spigot.

We kneeled beside it, and Alex ripped a piece of his shirt and held it under the cold water. When it was saturated, he began to clean my face with gentle swipes. I found it hard to believe that the feathery touch came from a monster's movements.

"I used to do this for my mother," he said as he wiped the

cloth beneath my nose. Metallic water dripped into my mouth.

"What happened to her?" I asked.

His hand stopped its gentle downward motion. He seemed to consider saying more, but he changed his mind before the words could form. "We aren't pals, O. We don't need to talk about our pasts like we're building some kind of friendship here. Get that out of your head."

I looked away from him as he went back to cleaning my face in silence. When he'd washed away the blood, his fingers prodded at my sore nose. He ran his finger down the length of it, hovering over the bridge. When he put pressure on it, a deep ache rushed through my face, and I flinched.

"It's not broken. But that's going to hurt like a son of a bitch tomorrow."

"It hurts like a son of a bitch now," I muttered.

Alex stared at me as if he needed to say something but couldn't bring himself to do it. His lips twitched. "How far did he get?" he finally asked. "Did he fuck you?"

I shook my head. "I bit him before he could."

His jaw relaxed. "Good girl," Alex said as he pushed back wet strands of my hair. I waited for him to say more, but he didn't. He looked lost in his mind.

ALEXZANDER

MY ENTIRE BEING shook with anger. What I walked into was exactly what I had worried would happen. Gunnir's pants had been down, his cock out, and Ophelia's skirt had been lifted around her waist. I saw red when I witnessed it. What he'd done to Ophelia's face only added to my rage. Fucking barbarian. I needed to get her out of the basement. I hadn't heard anything about what I'd told her, which meant she'd kept it to herself. I wasn't in the mood to fuck her at that moment, but I needed to speak with her without drawing suspicion. The spigot was too close to the whore, but if I pulled Ophelia away to fuck her, we'd have more privacy. I couldn't exactly sit beside her and carry on a conversation.

My face hardened as I stood and dragged her to her feet. Water drenched the front of her outfit, allowing me to see the faint shadow of her nipples beneath the thin material. I turned her over and pushed her against the wall, eerily like my brother had. I pressed my hips into hers and lifted her skirt. Her panties were long gone, and I had no doubt who took them. Fucking Gunnir. When my zipper fell, she turned to argue.

"Alex, no," she whispered.

I ignored her pleas. I needed to. In some warped and twisted way, this was for her.

She hardly flailed against me. She'd become so accustomed to being my toy. I knew she hated it, but she wasn't fighting as much, which was almost disappointing. I spit in my hand, but I didn't rub it on my cock like I usually did. Instead, I reached between her legs and rubbed the warm saliva against her pussy. Her thighs tensed against my touch. I pulled her hips toward me and pushed inside her, groaning as her heat embraced me. It was hard to focus on anything aside from how good she felt once I was inside her, but I had to.

Focus, I told myself. I dropped my head to the curve of her neck. She smelled like captivity, and I found myself wanting to give her a bath. I liked how she'd smelled when we first brought her here. When she smelled like sweet innocence.

"Remember what I said to you?" I whispered as I curled my hips and thrust into her. She nodded. "Did you say anything?" I asked. She shook her head. "Good girl, O."

My hips slammed against her, and unintentional

whimpers left her mouth. "Can you explain more now?" she whispered, and I answered with a hard thrust.

"Don't say a thing," I said.

She went silent, dropping her head to the basement wall.

"I want you in my room. I want to keep you safe from everyone except me." I reached down and gripped her hip. "I'm going to leave a nail by the spigot, right by the drain trench. I need you to try to kill me again."

She shook her head.

"If you don't, you'll be left down here at Gunnir's disposal. He's going to get inside you. I know it, and so do you."

A tear rolled down her cheek and hit the hand I'd laced across her chest.

"You aren't going to kill me, no matter how much you want to," I said, certain of the words coming out of my mouth. Killing me meant belonging to Gunnir. "Can you do that for me?"

She remained motionless while I thrust into her, my head still buried in her neck so my breath rolled over her ear. Then I felt her nod.

"Good girl," I whispered, dropping my hands to either side of her head and fucking her with slow, deep thrusts that pushed her against the rough wall in front of her. "I'm going to come," I growled, loud enough for the whore to hear.

Ophelia dropped her head forward and let me fill her with a rough stutter of my hips. I turned her around. She looked so confused, as if I was putting her in a trap, but I genuinely needed her to try to kill me if I wanted my idea to have a chance of working.

I pushed my fingers inside her, coating them with my come. Her lip curled at my touch, and she dropped back her head and squeezed her eyes closed. I lifted my hand to her mouth, and she shook her head as I touched my fingers to her lips. "Open up," I commanded. She tightened her lips, but I held her nose. She struggled against me until her lungs forced her mouth to open, and I shoved my fingers inside. She lowered her teeth on my fingers. I thought she'd bite me, and I was ready to punch her myself if she did. Instead, she loosened her grasp and let me pull my fingers out of her mouth.

I shook my hand like I needed to wash the come from my skin. My come didn't bother me, but it gave me a reason to approach the spigot. I washed my hands with the soap hovering on the lip of the wall. With my body turned to block the whore's view, I reached into my pocket and tossed down a long, rusty nail. My eyes met Ophelia's once more before I dried my hands on my pants and zipped them up.

I didn't have the time to give her a rundown of any type of plan, so I'd need to keep my eyes open for whatever she conjured up in that pretty head. I'd be back for her later that night.

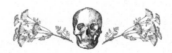

I PUT our dinner plates in the sink, and Gunnir sat back with a satiated groan. He patted his belly, wiped at a stain on the front of his overalls, and licked his fingers.

"Guess you're too comfortable to bring them their dinner?" I said with an annoyed huff.

Gunnir laughed. "I couldn't walk down the stairs if I tried right now."

The first part of my plan went off without a hitch: feed Gunnir until he was nearly in one of his food comas. That was easy enough to accomplish; if I kept feeding him, he'd keep eating.

I separated some beef stew into two bowls and carried them downstairs. The basement door creaked as I closed it behind me. The girls were huddled in their spots, tense with fear, but they both relaxed a little when they saw it was me.

I handed a bowl of stew to the whore first. Her eyes blazed with hunger the minute she smelled the food. We fed them, but dinner was their only hearty meal of the day. Gunnir worried they'd get fat on their chains if we offered more than that, which was ironic. There was certainly no chain keeping Gunnir from expanding his waistline, one meal at a time.

When I brought the bowl to Ophelia and held it out, her eyes rolled up my body. She had a look I'd never seen from her, not even the night she wrapped the chain around my throat. Granted, I only saw her eyes for a moment before she attacked me, but this time she was staring into my fucking soul. She rose to her knees and lifted a hand to grab the bowl I held toward her. I raised my eyebrow at her as she dropped her gaze and took her dinner from me. I saw the flash of movement a second before she came at my thigh with the nail. The bowl fell from her hand and shattered against the concrete. I caught her wrist as the nail's pointed tip tore through my jeans and narrowly missed puncturing my skin. I leapt onto her. With the force she was putting behind each stab, I realized how wrong I'd been. She meant it.

"Fucking bitch!" I yelled as I fought her flailing legs and arms. Anger darkened her eyes, and she'd have gone for my throat if given the chance. I grabbed her wrist and pinned it to the ground. "I should break your arm for that."

The struggle caused me to harden. Focus evaporated as she writhed beneath me and sent blood straight to my dick. I glanced at the whore, whose eyes were wide with surprise. I had to do something to punish Ophelia to make this look real.

I ripped the nail from her hand and threw it across the basement. It pinged against the wall and rolled along the floor. I kept her pinned on her back and put my weight into my hand as I wrapped it around her throat. My other hand worked off my jeans.

"Big mistake," I said.

Before she could protest, I pushed my cock past her lips. Even though she felt so fucking good, I couldn't take a moment to enjoy her mouth around me. This was a punishment. I thrust my hips forward until snot spewed from her nose. She made an ungodly sound beneath me, and I felt the lurch of her throat as she gagged. I kept my dick there until her chest heaved. I pulled out just in time, and she turned her head to vomit. Her eyes watered, and fat tears dripped down her face as she coughed. I let her catch her breath for a moment before I forced her down and did it again, making her take every inch of me until her stomach heaved and she brought up bile.

"Fuck you," I snarled as I forced myself into her mouth once more. Her teeth scraped my dick as she choked on me. She was covered in sweat and tears when I pulled out of her mouth a final time. I tucked myself away and went to the plate on the wall. I dug in my pocket, pulled out the key, and unfastened the lock from the anchor. Next I removed her ankle shackle. Panting and breathless, she remained still as I wrapped the chain around her neck and locked it on itself.

"Please," she pleaded.

"Too late for begging." I took the tail of the chain and dragged her toward the stairs. She gripped the metal links to keep them from sawing into her neck as she tried to keep up with me, and I slammed the basement door after I yanked her onto the main floor.

Gunnir's eyes snapped to me. "What the hell happened?" he asked.

I led Ophelia to his feet and pushed her to the ground. "She tried to kill me again," I said as I pointed toward the rip in my pants. "Tried to stab me with a goddamn nail." In the light, I saw the bruise that spread like a butterfly along her cheeks. The anger in her face had melted away, and her body trembled with fear.

Gunnir's eyes jumped to mine.

"I told you," I said with a sharp rise in my voice. "They aren't good down there together. I can't keep worrying about being killed in my own goddamn house."

"What do you want us to do, then?" Gunnir asked. "I know I said we shouldn't separate them, but I don't think there's any other way."

I stopped and thought for a moment, even though I already knew what I needed to say. It had to be Gunnir's idea, and it was, but I had to pretend to consider it. "I can put her on the hook in my room for now. The bitches can't talk if they're on separate floors."

"You ruin everything!" Gunnir screamed at Ophelia, slamming his fist on the table. She flinched at his words. "Fucking whores."

I dragged Ophelia toward my room and closed the door behind us. I moved the bedside table and chained her to the plate on the floor. She slunk against the wall like a scared animal, her lips still red and puffy from my assault. I sat on my bed and wiped the sweat from my forehead.

"That was fucking excessive," I whispered toward her as I rubbed the gaping rip in my pants.

Her eyes rose to meet mine. "It wasn't excessive enough."

I shook my head. "You meant that, didn't you?"

"Every stab."

"Well, you're out of the fucking basement."

Her eyes dropped to the floor, and she wrapped her arms around her knees.

My plan worked, but for how long? What would I even do with her in my bedroom? I knew what I wanted to do. She was still a captive, after all, and she'd be treated as one.

CHAPTER NINE

OPHELIA

Alex had locked me in his bedroom. Even though it was better than the basement, in ways, it was worse. Being stuck in a room with him didn't seem like the best idea. I'd be at his disposal, something to use when he wished. It saved me from being alone with Gunnir, but was it really much better?

I looked around the old bedroom but found little to catch my eye. A full-size bed with a rusted metal frame stood in the center of the room. A dresser pressed against the wall, half covering a small closet with a broken door. The bedside table wobbled on uneven legs by the wall. Then, of course, there was me, the new centerpiece.

Even though his room didn't smell like piss, sex, and body odor, there was no spigot to clean up and no bucket to use the bathroom in. I held my bladder until it throbbed because I had no other choice. I was forced to wait until Alex came back into the room to release me from the anchor so I could pee.

I rolled the chain along the floor, like I'd done in the basement. It was the equivalent of a trapped animal pacing the wall of their cage. It was repetitive behavior to comfort my ailing mind. I leaned against the wall and sighed.

The door unlocked and I looked up as Alex came into the room. His lips were tight. "Gunnir isn't happy with this new arrangement," he said with a shake of his head. "He thinks I brought you up here so I could fuck you more often."

"Is that not why?" I asked in a harsh whisper.

His eyes narrowed on me. "You're being ungrateful."

I cut my gaze and stared at an ant dancing circles around a hole in the hardwood floor. It would stop and start again, seeming to realize it was getting nowhere fast but having no clue how to stop its spiral. I never related to an insect more in my life.

"I didn't bring you up here to fuck you more," he said as he sat on the bed. The springs squeaked, and the antiquated air that puffed toward me told me he hadn't washed those sheets in a very long time, if ever. "I did it to keep Gunnir's hands off you. Ungrateful bitch. If I only did this to fuck you more, don't you think I'd have laid you on this bed and taken you by now?"

I nodded without looking up at him. "Is Sam okay?"

His lips tightened. "She will be."

I felt the guilt as his words ripped through me. Sam had become collateral damage in a plan she'd had no part of. I shivered as I realized that Gunnir probably did awful things to her during a punishment she never deserved.

"She didn't do anything, and you know that," I said as my icy gaze rose to meet him.

Alex scoffed. "You need to learn what to do to survive, O. She'd throw you under Gunnir if she knew it would get her out of that basement."

"No, she wouldn't. She didn't even when she could have."

"You don't know what captivity does to you, do you? I

know. I've lived it myself. Eventually, the only thing you have to care about is yourself."

"Sam isn't like that," I said with a shake of my head. "And neither am I."

"You're here, aren't you?"

I turned away from him. "I have to pee," I whispered.

He grabbed my chain, unfastened the lock that anchored me to the floor, and dragged me toward the bedroom door. I looked around before I crossed the hall, searching for the sounds of Gunnir or Sam. The house was eerily quiet. Alex led us into the bathroom and closed the door behind us.

I stared at him. "I can't go with you here," I said.

"You'll have to."

I took a deep breath, lifted my skirt, and sat on the wobbly toilet. His eyes never left me as I peed, and my cheeks flamed hot with embarrassment. My gaze moved from a hole in the wall and landed on the shower. For a moment, I forgot I was peeing in front of him as the shower became my new obsession.

"Can I shower?" I asked, the drool of excitement filling the dry void beneath my tongue.

Alex put his hand to his chin. I was certain I looked like a mess, with my matted, greasy hair and the blood covering my skin and clothes.

"I guess it wouldn't hurt anything," he said. He walked past me and turned on the shower. The water rumbled through the pipes behind the wall before an uneven torrent fell from the showerhead. Alex reached into a cupboard and pulled out a towel. "It's not a hot shower."

I nodded. If I could clean myself—actually clean myself, not a sponge bath down in the basement—I didn't care.

Alex leaned against the door and watched me. I wanted to ask him to leave, but the way he leaned against the wood, so sure and focused, I knew it would have been futile. My fingers worked open the buttons on my uniform top, and his eyes dropped to my chest. My cheeks burned hotter with every inch the fabric spread. The swells of my breasts peeked from the opening. I tried to turn away, but he cleared his throat. There was no choice but to face him as I exposed more of my skin. More of me that I didn't want him to see. I stripped the rest of my uniform off, and his gaze burned through me. His muscles twitched around his mouth as he fought back a smirk. My eyes dropped to the strained zipper at the front of his pants. I was surprised he hadn't already pounced on me. He had so much more control than his brother.

I wrapped my arm around my chest and tried to hide my breasts. My other hand dropped to my crotch, keeping myself covered as I backed toward the shower. I opened the shower curtain and climbed inside, nearly slipping when I tried to step over the high side of the tub. When I went to close the curtain, Alex made a noise in his throat.

"Leave it open."

"Water will get everywhere," I said, which was so fucking dumb to care about, but it just came out.

"I don't give two fucks about the water. I want to watch you."

I put my head beneath the cool water, and it plastered my hair to my back and shoulders. It was hard to ignore the sound of his falling zipper as I tried to wash the grime away. Soon, the sound of him jerking off overpowered all other sounds. I was too ashamed to look at him, but I felt the fire of his stare over my shoulder as I cleaned my body. I thought Alex was the more refined one between the two, but as he growled and selfishly came to my body, I was more certain they were one and the same.

"Turn toward me, O," Alex said with a growl.

The cold water pelted my shoulder and pebbled my skin with goosebumps.

"I won't fuck you if you give me what I want," he urged.

I turned around, letting him see the intimate parts of me I'd tried to hide. "What do you want?" I asked, though I knew. I knew from the twist in my gut what he wanted. My eyes dropped to his hand around his cock, one hand pushing his jeans to the side as he stroked the long length of his dick with the other.

"Touch yourself." He groaned and dropped his head against the door.

"Alex . . . please . . ."

"You can make yourself come or I can fuck you, whichever you'd prefer."

I sighed and put my fingers between my legs. I tried to think of my ex-boyfriend and pretend it was his hand. I imagined his tongue on me as I stroked my clit. I closed my eyes and bathed in the touch of anyone else I'd slept with, because even the worst was better than this. It did nothing. I was numb. No amount of fantasizing could help me feel less stared at. Less watched. Any less violated.

When I rubbed more furiously, a frustrated exhale escaped my throat and sent droplets of water flying forward.

Alex stopped stroking himself. "Do I disgust you that much?" he asked as he stepped toward me. My body trembled, not from the cold water, but because he approached me with a hard dick.

I shook my head and kept my eyes closed. "What you've done to me disgusts me."

"Well, that was a chance for you to get some pleasure from this little setup that so unfairly favors me," Alex snarled as he went to rip the curtain across the rod.

I caught it and held it open. I swallowed hard and tried to get back in his good graces. I didn't need to feel the pleasure to make him think I was feeling it. The old me used to be an ace student in theater classes. I could act.

I kept my eyes on him as I rubbed between my legs once more, curling my fingers over my clit as he started to stroke himself again. His breath caught in his throat as I moaned and bucked my hips forward. I wasn't sure if he knew I was faking it as I raised the other hand to my chest and squeezed my breast.

"Fuck, O," he groaned as his strokes quickened. "I want to put my mouth on you."

I didn't want that. I shook my head and lifted my leg, putting my foot on the edge of the tub, giving him a better view of my spread pussy. I pushed my fingers inside myself and moaned. The bead of come dripping from his head and the ragged tempo of his strokes made me certain he was going to bust. I would get him off before he could put his mouth on me.

"Come with me," I told him as I dropped my head back and fucked myself. I faked my orgasm, and he didn't hesitate before he stepped toward me and fisted my hair. He pushed me down to my knees.

"Lean back," he said as he pumped his hand slower, squeezing the base of his cock to stop himself from coming before he had me where he wanted me. I craned my neck and he stroked himself above my face. His warm come painted my lips, and I fought the urge to gag. He rubbed his come into my cheeks, using a finger to push some of it into my mouth. The attempt to fight a gag was futile the moment the salty taste hit my tongue. "Good fucking girl," he moaned as he stroked against my cheek.

I didn't like that he came on my face like he owned me, but I hated him coming inside me more. Stroking his dick to me was better than fucking me. For another day, my pussy was safe, but my face and mouth had not been so lucky.

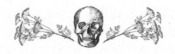

Alexzander

I LOOKED DOWN AT HER. My come coated her sweet face. Her big eyes looked up at me, and for a moment, I almost forgot what we'd done hadn't been consensual. She didn't want any of it, and I knew she faked her fucking orgasm, but I only cared about spilling my load on her face.

I tucked myself away as I backed toward the door. She got out of the shower, clean and looking even sweeter as her dark hair adhered to her neck. I wanted her so fucking bad, even though my balls were empty. I was obsessed. Fucking obsessed with her. And the more I thought about it, the less I thought I'd made the best decision by bringing her to my room. It was important I didn't just fuck her all the time, because Gunnir would throw her ass right back in the basement. I had to prove it was for the betterment of us, not just me.

"Don't get dressed," I said as I dragged her across the hall, her naked body wrapped in nothing more than a thin towel.

Her eyes clenched when I shut the door, and I knew what she thought I planned to do to her. I wanted to, believe me, I wanted to, but instead of putting a hand on her, I reached behind my dresser, into the closet, and grabbed a flannel shirt. The adrenaline coursing through her at the thought of being taken again sent her into a full-body tremble, so I dressed her. I buttoned every button, right up to the top, slowly hiding her skin with every inch my fingers rose. I stepped back and stared at her.

She looked so fucking sexy in my shirt. Her breasts pushed against the fabric, testing the strength of the top three buttons. She was still naked from the waist down, so I reached into a drawer and handed her a pair of my boxers. Her lip curled at the sight of them, but she refused to let me help her put them on. They would feel better than that skirt, though. They'd protect her sensitive skin from the floor. She could thank me later.

I attached her chain to the anchor on the floor and sat on the edge of my bed to watch her step into the boxers. She curled her body to hide what I'd already seen and what I would see again if I wanted to. Once she got them on, she sat on the floor in the corner and leaned against the wall.

Now what? Smart or not, I'd done it. I'd gotten my plaything into my room, and now I didn't know what to do with her. Gunnir was probably asleep by now, and I didn't want to risk waking him by forcing myself on her. She'd scream. She'd kick, flail, and fight. I forced those images out of my mind. It excited me too much.

My eyes went to the closet, and I got an idea. When I stood from the bed, her muscles tensed and she pulled her knees to her chest. I didn't tell her to relax. It wouldn't do any good. She knew why she was here in this house, and I wouldn't sell her lies to offer her comfort. My brother and I weren't the same, but we were still cut from the same cloth.

I went to the closet and pulled a crumpled blanket from the floor. I placed it in front of her and unfolded the threadbare edges until I'd revealed the tattered cardboard box containing the game of checkers.

"Do you know how to play?" I asked.

She tore her eyes from me long enough to look at the box, then she nodded.

"Good. I tried to teach Gunnir how to play when we were little, but he couldn't get the hang of it." I pulled the board from the box. The seam through the middle had ripped long ago, but the game could still be played on the two sections. I arranged the black and red pieces on the board, red in front of her and black in front of me. I always played the black pieces because they got to move first.

Halfway through the first game, she finally spoke. "Why do you keep this hidden in your closet?"

I shrugged my shoulders and captured one of her pieces. "Gunnir wouldn't like it. He'd burn it if he found it."

My move had opened up an opportunity for her, and she jumped two of my checkers, capturing both. "Why?"

When she'd asked about my mother in the basement, I hadn't wanted to talk about it, but what could it hurt now? It wasn't as if she could tell someone else what we discussed. "My mother used to play this with me, and he doesn't like any reminders of her because he thinks she made me soft." I pushed one of my pieces ahead on the board.

"You don't seem very soft to me," she muttered.

"It's your move," I said.

She studied the board. "You still haven't told me what happened to your mom. I can only assume she died." Her hand moved toward a red checker, but she pulled her finger back and kept thinking. "If so, that's something we have in common."

"Did your mother kill herself?"

She pushed one of her checkers forward, opening up an opportunity for me. I jumped her piece and took it away. "In a way, I guess," she said. "She chose to stay with my dad, and he's good at removing your will to live."

My move had left me vulnerable to another double jump. I didn't have many pieces left on the board once she took those two. As I made my next move, I considered telling her how my mom died, but I didn't want to give her any ideas. "Do you want to talk about your dad?" I asked instead, but she shook her head.

We had more in common than she realized.

Chapter Ten

Ophelia

Alex came into the room the next morning after not speaking to me since we finished our game of checkers the night before. He'd given me a blanket to sleep on and one of the stained pillows from his bed so I wouldn't have to rest my head on the dirty hardwood. I'd tried to be grateful and not consider what could have caused the stains. With a frustrated breath, he wiped a hand through his thick hair.

"What's the matter?" I asked, drawing his attention to me. I was trying to reach through to him as one human to another, but it backfired the moment he looked at me and his eyes narrowed. I was better off keeping quiet and not drawing him to me at all.

"Gunnir's pissed I wouldn't play with the whore. Her face is fucking rearranged, and I just . . ." He shook his head, cutting off the rest of the sentence. He paced, his body trembling with anger.

"Is there anything I can do to help?" I asked. The wood

rubbed against my skin through the thin blanket as I sat up on my knees.

"Not when I'm frustrated like this. I'm sick of the goddamn fighting that started when you got here."

Shots fired.

I sat back on my heels. I didn't choose to be here. The fighting had nothing to do with me and everything to do with them. Still, I needed to diffuse this situation before he took out his frustration on me. He continued pacing, the rage growing in his eyes with every step.

"He only wants me to use her so that he can use *you*," he said through gritted teeth. The veins on his neck stood out like thick wires filled with electricity. He stopped pacing and turned to face me. "Come lay on your back." Alex gestured toward the bed, and I did as I was told.

As I crawled onto the mattress, the time we'd spent together last night seemed like a distant memory. For a moment, we had been two people playing a game of checkers and talking about our pasts. Now I wasn't a person to him anymore. I was a thing to use.

Alex gripped my shoulders and tugged me toward the edge of the mattress until my head dropped over the side. I embraced the sweet dizziness as blood rushed to my brain. If I was lucky, I'd pass out before he even got started. Alex wound his fingers through my hair and cushioned my neck. With one hand, he tugged down his sweatpants and his cock fell in front of my face. He rubbed the tip along my lips and when I didn't open my mouth, he shook me by my hair.

"Don't fuck with me right now, O. I'm not in the mood."

I spread my lips, allowing him inside my mouth. He forced his way to the back of my throat, and I fought back a gag. He groaned and gripped my hair tighter, pushing his hips forward before drawing back and letting me catch my breath. He looked down at me. The rage in his green eyes had dissipated to little more than a flicker. Some other emotion lurked there now, growing until it smothered his anger.

It was his desire.

For me.

Visceral noises left him as he pushed himself into my mouth again. His hand wrapped around the back of my neck, holding me steady as he leaned forward and worked my mouth harder.

"Such a good girl," he groaned.

I hated him, but the way he called me a good girl made me swell with unwanted pride. I didn't want to be good for him, but I felt a sick sense of accomplishment for having pleased him.

He pulled out but instead of pushing his cock into my mouth, he slid his shaft up my nose and brought his balls to my lips. I didn't need him to tell me what he wanted me to do. I drew his balls into my mouth and sucked. The urge to bite down on them was a difficult one to fight. I imagined the pain it would cause. What if I ripped them clean off? It would ruin all he was.

A feeling between my legs cut off my violent thoughts. It was a soft touch, something I'd never expected from him. He slipped a hand down the boxers and rubbed me. I wanted to pull his balls from my mouth and ask him why he was touching me. What did he think he was doing?

I tried to ignore his hand between my legs as he rubbed me. I expected the clumsy touch of an inexperienced lover, but his fingers understood my body. I pulled my thighs together to stop him from drawing pleasure out of me, and he removed his balls from my mouth.

"You don't like when I touch you?" he asked, circling my clit with his fingertips.

I shook my head.

"Why not?"

"Because I don't like you," I whispered. I half expected him to get angry at my honesty, but he sighed as if he understood.

"You don't have to like me to come," he said, an eerie calmness in his tone. "I know what you did in the bathroom was fake."

How did he know that? How did he know anything about pleasing a woman?

I tried to pull away from his touch again. "Please don't," I said. I didn't want him to touch me, and he didn't need to. He could just use me. That's it.

"Gunnir wouldn't make someone come. He couldn't, not even if he tried." His hand tightened around my neck. "I learned how to make them come, even when they fought it. Don't fight me, Ophelia."

I shivered at the words so laced with subtle threats. He was trying to tell me to be thankful it was him between my legs and not Gunnir. I was already thankful for that.

I pinched my thighs closed and put his cock back in my mouth.

"Suit yourself," he said as he drew his hand from between my legs, dropped his weight onto it, and fucked my face.

I fought back gags as his relentless thrusts pummeled my throat. His hips finally stuttered, and his warm come hit the back of my tongue. He pressed his hips deep into me so I could neither swallow nor breathe. I choked, and his come shot out of my nose and burned my sinuses. I tapped his thigh, trying to get him to pull out of me, but he just kept me there, choking on his dick.

He pulled his cock from my throat, and as I gasped for air, he leaned toward my ear. "Next time I get the urge to please you, fucking let me or I'll drown you in my come," he whispered.

Letting his fingers work me would have been exponentially better than this. I really needed to rethink my strategy.

ALEXZANDER

I HANDLED THAT POORLY. I knew I had. It hurt me to look at her, with her lips still puffy and cheeks flaming red. I wanted to make her come. That was all I wanted to do, and she just fought me on it. Kept pushing me until I did what I did. She wasn't like the other women. I made them come because I could, but I wanted to make her come because I wanted her to feel good. I was being selfless, and she fucking poked me about it. So I became even more selfish. I became my fucking brother.

Fuck.

There was no amount of apologizing I could do at that point. I saw it in her eyes. She was more upset about what I'd done than when I fucked her. Maybe I should stick to doing what I knew best, the force and control I grew up learning before I could even read.

I left her in the bedroom and went to the basement. Gunnir was still using his whore, but I knew he was almost done. His hands were digging into the table as his thrusts quickened.

"How was she?" he asked.

"I didn't do anything with her," I lied. I didn't want him to think I brought her to my room to use her. That's not why I wanted her in that room. It was to protect her from him. Using her was just a bonus.

"Then what's that stain on the front of your pants?" he asked.

I looked down and realized she had splashed my come back onto me. *Well, shit.* "She was being mouthy, so I took her throat."

Gunnir grabbed Sam's mouth, hooking his fingers and tugging on her lips. "But her mouth isn't good enough for you?" Through red, glazed-over eyes, she looked at me with a desperation I'd never noticed before.

"Fuck off, Gunnir. I didn't plan on using Ophelia's mouth either."

Gunnir groaned as he finished. He pulled out his wet dick and wiped himself with a dirty hand before hiking up his overalls. He smacked Sam's face, making her whimper and cover the bloody cuts on her cheeks.

He'd tried to get her to admit to her part in the attack by cutting into her face and chest, nearly skinning her in some areas. She never admitted to anything because she hadn't been the mastermind. I had. She didn't even throw me under the bus. She just took her undeserved punishment with a stoicism I could respect.

In a way, she reminded me of myself. I used to take the blame for Gunnir sometimes, and The Man would whip me until I bled. He'd dip the whip in buckets of water so it would rip through my skin and sting even more. For some reason, I'd felt the need to protect Gunnir, even though his evil surpassed mine. Once he'd surpassed The Man, I let Gunnir take his own beatings.

Gunnir squeezed my shoulder and told me to come upstairs. I followed the sound of his denim scraping together as he walked.

"You know what I was thinking?" he said as he plopped down at the kitchen table with a satiated groan.

"What?"

"I think we should have her fine little ass cook for us. Like

Mama used to do. I'd love to watch her bending over to do the dishes."

It made sense. Ophelia needed a job if she was going to be upstairs, but that also meant putting her on display for him if I did what he was asking. But maybe cooking wouldn't be so bad. I'd be here to step in if needed. "I'll bring her to the kitchen and let her cook."

Gunnir's eyes widened. "I've got the perfect outfit for it!" He heaved himself from the table and went toward his room, returning moments later with a maid outfit. He'd picked it up months ago, after a Halloween clearance sale, and planned to make the whore wear it. I'd forgotten all about it until now. I wished he had too. I fought the urge to tell him to fuck off with that, but he was suspicious already, and I couldn't give him more ammo. I just shrugged, and he tossed it to me.

I went to my room and held the skimpy fabric in front of Ophelia. She looked up at me with wide eyes.

"What's this?"

"Gunnir wants you to wear it while you make breakfast."

"You're fucking kidding me," she said, her mouth gaping.

"I'm not."

Her lips tightened and she scooped up the thin material. "Well, can you at least leave me to get dressed?"

I cocked my head at her because she already knew the answer to that. "Go on," I told her.

She stood and started to unbutton her shirt. When she turned away, I growled. "In front of me, O. You know better."

She turned around and continued to undo the buttons until I could see the swells of her breasts. Fuck, she was gorgeous. And she was mine.

She threw the white lacy strap over her neck and tugged the cheap material around her midriff. She turned around and pointed to her bare back. I helped her fasten the lacy strings, tying them like I tied my shoes—real slow, with the rabbit running under the tree.

She replaced my boxers with the black panties that had a cute little apron hanging in the front. Her hands went behind her, trying to cover the cuffs of her ass. She looked good enough to eat, and that made me nervous. If I wanted to lay her out and have her for breakfast, I had no doubt Gunnir would too. She was untouchable, and nothing screamed "touch me" more than something you couldn't.

I unlocked her chain and brought her to the kitchen. Gunnir devoured her body with his eyes, focused and slow, taking her all in. Her cheeks flushed redder than when I made her choke on my dick.

"Make me eggs like you did in the diner," Gunnir commanded.

Ophelia looked at me. "I never made the food," she whispered.

I leaned toward her. "I know that, but he doesn't."

She tried to back toward the kitchen once I released her chain.

"Nuh uh. I want to see you walk away," Gunnir snapped. He spun his large finger in the air, demanding she give him a view of her from every angle.

With closed eyes and tight lips, she turned and dropped her hands from her ass. Gunnir hooted and hollered, and I was certain he'd get out of the chair and pounce on her. But he didn't. He just licked his lips and rubbed the crotch of his overalls.

Ophelia obediently went to the fridge and grabbed a carton of eggs and began to break them into a pan on the stove. Gunnir liked them over easy, and I liked them soft scrambled. I wasn't sure if she'd remember, but I hoped she would. I sat at the table and watched her cook, keeping one eye on my brother.

Gunnir unclipped the strap of his overalls, and the denim fell past the swollen gut hanging below his dirty white shirt. His eyes darted over her body as she worked. Each time she stirred the eggs, her breasts jiggled. Each time she switched from one leg to the other, her hips shifted in a way that made her ass poke out. Gunnir stroked absentmindedly as he sat at the table with me, his stubby cock disappearing with the slightest movement of his hand. If there was a god, he'd graced both Gunnir and The Man with tiny dicks so they did less damage to the women. I'd gotten lucky in that department. I could hurt them so much more if I wasn't as gentle as I was. I wasn't always so in control of how I took them, and I'd done my fair share of damage in my younger days, when sex was still so new and exciting.

It ate away at me, the way he rubbed himself and drooled over Ophelia, but what could I do? If I made a fuss, he'd want her back in the basement, and I couldn't protect her there. It wasn't that I was afraid of him. He might have been bigger, but I had more muscle. And brains. I didn't want it to come to that, though. We were all we had in the world, and when Ophelia and the whore were gone, we'd still be here. Together.

My stomach tightened. The thought of a day when Ophelia wouldn't be here anymore didn't sit well with me, but what else would I do with her? I thought of my mother, chained to the bedroom, frail and miserable. I didn't want that for Ophelia.

What did I want for her?

Skin rubbed skin as Ophelia bent over to scrape the eggs onto a plate. He masturbated faster and harder, and I worried he'd rip the damn thing off in his excitement. Ophelia's eyes widened when she turned around and saw him beating off to her, and I thought she'd surely drop the plates of food. That would have been a mistake. Gunnir only liked one thing more than the girls, and it was food.

I threw Ophelia a quick shake of my head, trying to tell her not to acknowledge him. She did her best to ignore him, setting a plate of scrambled eggs in front of me and runny, yolk-covered eggs in front of Gunnir. She even grabbed the bottle of ranch from the fridge and set it beside my plate.

His eyes left hers as they went to the food. His tongue popped out of his mouth and his strokes slowed. "Look in the fridge," Gunnir said, grasping her forearm before she could move away from him. "There's a mayo jar on the bottom shelf. Bring it over here."

I knew where Gunnir was going with this, and I didn't like it.

She did as he instructed and pulled the jar from the fridge with a grimace. The slightly yellowed mixture in that jar wasn't mayonnaise.

"Get on your knees," he said, beginning to stroke himself again.

She shook her head and I had to intercept before she escalated the situation. Gunnir would do something far worse if she said no, and what he had planned was better than him taking her mouth or pussy. I kicked out her knees and she fell to the ground, still gripping the jar.

Gunnir licked his lips. "Open the jar and hold it between your tits."

Ophelia looked at me, using her eyes to plead for help. She didn't realize I was saving her by encouraging her to go along with this. I looked away until I heard the lid come off the jar. When I looked back, she was gagging and holding the jar between her breasts.

He stroked his dick faster, his glassy eyes alternating between her chest and the eggs on the plate. With a heavy groan, he came, squirting his load into the jar. Her throat clenched and bobbed. I thought she'd lose her stomach contents this time, but she managed to soften her expression and settle.

"Put that back in the fridge and get started on the dishes while the men eat," Gunnir commanded after he'd fastened his overalls in place.

She nodded and rose to her feet, scurrying to the fridge to rid herself of the come collection. At the sink, she washed her hands as if she'd touched raw sewage. In a way, I guess she had. She grabbed the pan and scrubbed, fighting back gloss in her eyes with every stroke of the sponge. I ate my breakfast, done perfectly, just as I liked it.

"Can I go to the bathroom?" she asked me as she dried her hands on the ripped towel we kept by the sink.

I nodded and led her down the hall. There was little hesitation as she raced to the toilet and when she was done, her eyes bore into mine. "Why'd you let him do that?"

I shook my head. "Don't question me, O. I know my brother better than you do. If you'd fought him on it, he'd have made you pay. He'd have taken more."

A shiver ran down her spine. "How long has he been collecting his . . ." She couldn't bring herself to finish the sentence.

"A few months now," I said with a shrug. "He wanted me to do it too, and I did for a while, but I stopped after a few weeks because I didn't see the point in it. Just don't drink from the Coke bottle by the ranch dressing in the fridge."

She washed her hands, and I dragged her back to the bedroom and locked her chain. "Thank you for breakfast," I told her as I pushed her clothes toward her.

She pulled them closer and clutched them to her chest. As I walked away, her soft voice drifted to me from across the room. "Thank you for helping me."

CHAPTER ELEVEN

OPHELIA

I was living in the burning flames of hell's playground, and I was the devil's toy. The worst part? I'd grown to like being around him. Or used to it, at least. Like a dog waiting for her master, I sat in my corner, anticipating his return. I wanted his attention, even if it was for all the wrong reasons. It was weird because I had enjoyed the loneliness at my father's house, but isolation in *this* house was driving me mad. I wanted him to talk to me, and I wanted him to keep me safe from his brother.

He came into the room after a few hours away and went to the closet. He pulled the hidden game of checkers from inside, and I couldn't help but smile at the look on his face. Playful and almost . . . sweet. Gunnir must have gone to bed, because he wouldn't have risked removing the game from its hiding place otherwise. He sat in front of me and laid out the broken board.

"Have you ever played chess?" I asked as he set out the pieces.

His eyes lit up. "I wanted to learn how to play that, but we only had checkers."

His childlike excitement made me smile. It was clear why his mother had preferred his company over Gunnir's. I could only imagine the horrors their mother went through and what pushed her to take her life. It was probably even worse than what I'd experienced. Actually, I was certain it was.

"What was your mother like?" I asked.

Alex seemed to disappear into his mind, probably trying to decide if this conversation was a good idea. After a moment, he got to his feet and grabbed a box from the closet. He put it on the floor and wrapped his long legs around it before pulling a picture from inside and handing it to me. The woman in the photograph had sandy brown hair like Alex, and the green shade to her eyes was the same, but that was about it. He must have inherited his other features from his father. I recognized the bed in the image, as well as the walls.

And the chain around her neck.

"That's my mother," he said with pride in his voice. He took the picture from me and gazed at it as he continued speaking. "She was good at checkers, just like you. And she could sing real sweet. The Man didn't like it when she sang, though, so she didn't do it often."

"The Man?" I asked. "Was that your father?"

His soft smile faded, but he didn't answer. "Did you live with your dad after your mom died?"

My lips tightened and I couldn't bring myself to respond.

"It's okay, you don't have to talk about it," Alex said as he moved a piece on the board, but telling me I didn't have to talk about it made me *want* to talk about it.

"My father is a bad person," I said with a shake of my head.

Alex's green eyes met mine, a mutual understanding growing between us. "Mine too."

I spotted a picture of a hand-traced turkey drawing, and I lifted it from the box before he could snatch it away. I turned it around and found his scrawled signature on the back. "Alexzander? With a z?" I looked at him over the edge of the paper.

"Yeah. It's Greek," he said. "It's your move."

I had doubts that any of them knew a damn thing about Greece, but I let it go and pushed one of my pieces across the board.

"You said your father *is* a bad person. Does that mean he's still alive?" he asked.

"Unfortunately," I muttered. "Though I don't know how long he'll last without me. He doesn't work, so our only income was what I brought in from the diner. He'll probably die from withdrawals when he can't afford his booze anymore."

"If he died, would that be a bad thing?"

I didn't answer him. I couldn't. It wasn't easy to admit I fantasized about my father's death on a daily basis. "Your move," I said.

He reached down and stopped, considered, then moved a piece, but he didn't place himself in a vulnerable position this time. He was improving.

"What about your dad?" I asked. "Where is he?"

"Gone," he said.

"Gone like he left or gone like he's dead?"

"Just gone, O. Drop it."

So I did. We played the rest of the game in silence. I captured the final black checker on the board, and Alex looked up at me with a tight scowl.

"Don't feel bad. I was on my school's chess team. We played checkers when we needed a change. I'm basically a professional," I said with a shrug. "Did you guys go to school?"

Alex laughed. "Do either of us seem schooled to you?"

I shrugged. "*You* kinda do."

"Thanks, but no. I'm self-taught. Gunnir didn't care to learn anything aside from the female anatomy," he said as he picked up the pieces and stacked them to put them away.

"How do you see yourself as different from him?" I knew I shouldn't have asked, but I did it anyway.

His body tensed. "I just am," he said with a shake of his head.

"You're both rapists."

A normal person would have been appalled by such an accusation, but Alex didn't even react. He knew what he was. Still, the guilt was evident from the downturn of his lips and the way he couldn't meet my eyes. He wasn't as soulless as he wanted me to believe.

He finished boxing up the checkers before he looked at me. "I'm a bad person, O. But I'm not the worst."

I turned my gaze to the door and scratched at my arm. Going so long between baths made my skin crawl. "Any chance I could shower tonight?"

Alex looked toward the door and sighed. "I guess it's okay. Just a quick one, though."

He unfastened my chain from the floor and led me to the bathroom, clutching the metal links in his hands to keep them from clanking together. I wished I could shower without the chain weighing down my neck. But I was glad I could shower at all. Sam wasn't so lucky. She was stuck with a spigot and the unending film of dirt that coated the walls and concrete. There was no way to get clean down there. I hoped she was okay. I wouldn't have known she was still alive if it weren't for Gunnir's heavy steps to and from the basement.

Cool water ran from the showerhead and pebbled my skin, and the cold chain froze me further. Alex's presence hovered just outside the shower, sitting on the closed toilet and waiting for me to be done. I just let the freezing water run over me because it was better than any alternative.

"Will you hurry up in there?" Alex said after a few minutes, and I could tell his face was leaning against his hand because his voice was muffled. "The water's cold now, isn't it?"

I made a noise that wasn't a yes or no, because the water was never *not* cold. A rustling noise came from outside the shower, and the curtain whipped open. I threw my arms over my chest and crotch, as if he hadn't seen it all already.

But I hadn't seen all of him. Not in the way he stood before me then. He was stark naked, without an ounce of bashfulness as he dropped my chain and took in my body with hungry eyes.

"Why?" I asked.

He shrugged. "I'm not letting you use up all the hot water," he said as he stepped past me to get beneath the spray.

"What? There's no hot water!" I said as I hugged myself tighter.

"This gets way colder."

I held my breath as his body grazed mine. I was done with the shower but when I tried to step out, he grabbed my chain. I sank back against the grungy wall and waited for him to finish.

My eyes trailed down his body. Above his muscles, long, thin scars crisscrossed his back, and small circular scars dotted his shoulders. I followed the marks down to his ass and back up again.

"Who did all that to you?" I asked.

"The Man," he said as he blew water from his lips. "Stop asking questions."

"Was he your father?"

Alex swung around and pushed his body into mine. He ripped my hands from my chest and my nipples hardened against his skin. "I said stop asking fucking questions."

"Sorry," I whispered as I cut my gaze.

His cock hardened against my lower stomach, and I closed my eyes and waited for him to take me, to teach me to keep my mouth shut. When my chain rattled, I opened my eyes and saw him step out of the shower. I was mostly surprised and relieved, but a tiny part of me felt a rising insecurity. Did I no longer interest him?

I flipped off the water and stepped out of the shower. He wrapped a towel around my wet skin, and without speaking, he led me toward the room.

He seemed mad at me. I shouldn't have pushed him. I was almost certain The Man was his father and if he was, he would have been the one to whip the sympathy out of Alex. Gunnir would have been the prodigal son. Sick and fucking twisted. Alex was sick too, but it reminded me more of someone who had been conditioned to the point of sickness.

Alex shoved me forward and closed the bedroom door behind me. Water dripped down his chest and nestled into the old towel around his waist. When he turned to look at me, his gaze burned through me.

"Alex . . ."

"Ophelia," he retorted. "I want you to stop asking questions about The Man. You don't need to know about him, and I don't need to talk about him. Is that clear?"

I nodded my head and adjusted the towel around my body.

His attention moved from my face to my chest, then went lower. His eyes darkened. "I want to make you come, O."

I shook my head and tightened the towel.

He stepped into me and fisted my damp hair, balling it at the nape of my neck. "Let me touch you."

"Why do you care if I get off?"

"I wonder that myself," he whispered as he leaned toward my lips.

My lungs struggled for air, making my chest rise against his. I didn't know what to do. He knew when I faked it, and if I refused, he'd probably force himself down my throat. I didn't want the burn of his come traveling through my sinuses again. But I *really* didn't want him to touch me. I didn't want to receive pleasure from any part of him.

Tears glossed my eyes. It was a no-win scenario.

With the towel still wrapped around his waist, Alex sat on the bed and parted his legs to create a space between them. He motioned me over, and I struggled to move toward him. My feet felt coated in lead. It took everything in me to take those few steps and sit between his legs.

My body trembled as his hands went to the front of my towel and spread it until the cool bedroom air prickled my skin. I was shaking, and I knew he felt every vibration against him. His fingers grazed my skin and his hand slid between my breasts. He brushed my nipples before squeezing them, forcing a whimper from my lips. As he cupped my breasts and played with my nipples, a low groan hummed in his chest. His mouth dropped to the curve of my neck and bit into my flesh.

"Fuck, O," he growled as he slid his hands down my stomach until he reached my slit. He rubbed me until the wetness gathered, then pinched my clit between his fingers. "I'm not going to fuck you, if that's what has you scared, so relax and enjoy."

I didn't relax. I tensed further as one hand squeezed my breast and his other hand worked my clit. It was so wrong. He was a horrible person, only trumped by Gunnir. He'd abducted me and caused me so much pain. He'd violated me.

And yet I found myself scooping my hips toward his touch.

"Good fucking girl." He kissed along my jaw before his lips found my mouth. "Come for me." He said the words like he'd never said them before in his life.

Whether I wanted it or not, his touch pulled pleasure from me. I relaxed my lips and allowed him to deepen the kiss. It couldn't hurt to—

The bedroom door flew open, and Gunnir stood in the doorway with his mouth hanging at the hinges. Alex pulled away from my mouth and covered me with my towel. I hugged myself and drew my legs toward my chest. He was still hard as he climbed out from behind me and stood up.

"The fuck, Alex?" Gunnir screamed.

"Gunnir," Alex said, as calmly as he could. "It's not what it looked like." Alex was talking as if he'd just got caught fucking Gunnir's wife or something. All he did was kiss me. He'd seen Alex kiss me in the basement, and he hadn't cared then.

"What were you doing between her legs? Why were you touching her like that? The Man—"

"Don't, Gunnir," Alex snapped, his jaw pulsing.

"We don't make them feel good, Alex. That's not what they're for!" Gunnir's voice raised another octave as he stepped toward his brother.

"*You* don't have to make them feel good, but I can do whatever I want with her. She's *mine*. If I want to play with her, then I'll play with her."

"Fucking pussy. Mama made you that way. Does she remind you of her, mama's boy?"

Gunnir grabbed the belt hanging on the door and walked toward me. He was on me before I could scoot away. His fingers coiled through my hair, and he yanked me from the bed. His other hand reached for the towel and snatched it away, leaving me bare in front of him. I went to cover my chest, but he grabbed my arms and ripped them away. I screamed for Alex, which just enraged Gunnir more. He pushed my chest to the dresser and forced my legs apart.

"They don't get to feel good," Gunnir snarled as he drew

his arm back and brought the folded leather down on my skin. I screamed out and tried to pull away. "Don't move, stupid bitch, or I'll put something worse inside you than either of our cocks."

Tears fell down my cheeks as I searched for Alex in the dresser mirror. He stood behind us, looking as stuck as I was. He was trying to figure a way out of this situation, but the desperation flitting through his eyes made me think there was no hope.

When Gunnir brought the belt down on me again, I dug my nails into the aged wood. A warm trail of blood dripped down my thigh, and I dropped my head and bit my arm so I wouldn't scream again. Over the heartbeat in my ears, I heard the unmistakable sound of a switchblade swinging free.

"Maybe I should just take off what makes her feel good, huh, Alex?" Gunnir goaded.

Whipping wasn't enough for him. He meant to do more damage. Irreparable damage. I tried to get away, but his weight pressed into me and held me fast.

Another sound overshadowed Gunnir's sick and twisted laugh—a gun being racked. He lifted his weight off my back and turned around, but I didn't need to turn. I could see my savior in the mirror. Alex stood with squared shoulders, his legs spread in a shooter's stance.

And the shotgun he held was aimed at his brother.

Gunnir dropped the belt. "Oh, little brother," he said through a weak laugh. "Big fucking mistake."

"We'll see," Alex snarled.

I dropped to the ground in a naked, bleeding mess. Tears soaked my cheeks, and I couldn't open my eyes. Only once I heard Gunnir's footsteps receding did I look up and see Alex unloading the shells and hiding them in a drawer.

"Fuck, O," he said. "I fucked up." There was a fear in his voice I'd never heard. He shoved the shotgun into the closet and sat back against the wall. "I only wanted to make you feel good. For once."

"Alex," I whispered.

He crawled closer and took my face in his hands. "You're fucked, O. And I'm sorry."

The fear in his voice proved I wasn't the only one who had to worry about Gunnir. That piece of shit had a scary hold on Alex too.

Chapter Twelve

Alexzander

The next day, Gunnir acted like nothing had happened. Like he hadn't threatened to cut Ophelia. Like I hadn't pulled a gun on him. It unnerved me. Normally when I pissed him off, he'd stomp around the house and pout and make life miserable for a few days. If he was acting like everything was fine and dandy, it meant he had something up his sleeve to make me pay for last night.

I'd just wanted to make her feel good. I wanted to feel her chasing my fingers instead of trying to get away from me. I liked that my dick responded to the scoop of her hips, and the soft moans that escaped her lips made me as hard as the crying and fighting. I loved that I didn't feel guilty for the erection because it wasn't for The Man's reasons.

But I had fucked up.

Gunnir would never accept anything aside from what The Man taught him, and that lesson had been simple: You caught them, fucked them in the most selfish ways, and got rid of them once you grew bored. Unlike Gunnir, I never had sex with them to hurt them. I just did it to please myself. And the way she bucked against my hand pleased me. I liked the soft pout of her lips as her eyes closed and the pleasure built inside her. Pleasure I created. When the moans she tried to hold back leaked from her lips, it did something to me. And now she would pay for it.

Gunnir would never understand the reasons why I wanted to touch her like that. I hardly understood it myself, but I tried to make it make sense. It was what I wanted, not what she wanted. He didn't see the way she resisted and pleaded for me to stop. He didn't hear me command her to sit between my legs and let me explore her body. Gunnir walked in only once she started to enjoy my touch. But that was enough to send him spiraling.

Ophelia stood by the stove, cooking dinner in her little maid outfit and trying to avoid looking at Gunnir. I couldn't help watching her because the full cuffs of her ass beneath her panties made my mouth water. I wanted to bury my face between her legs as she bent over the sink.

But why? Why would I want to do that?

Jesus, my head was off. We didn't eat them out. We never put our mouths on them like that. But Ophelia was so pure, and I wanted to devour her innocence and swallow every drop.

"Did you hear me?" Gunnir asked.

"What?" I said, breaking from the delicious thought of being on my knees behind Ophelia.

Gunnir laughed. "Holy fuck, girl. You got Alex here whipped as all get out." His lips tightened. "I said I'd like to have a party. Get the girls dressed all nice and pretty. Play music. Dance."

I didn't like the look in his eyes. His idea sounded innocent, but it wasn't.

Ophelia brought over the plates of baked chicken and steamed vegetables. Each step she took was accented by a wince. She still hurt from the whipping she'd received the night before. There was a subtle twitch of pain in her lips as she turned to walk away.

"Ah ah, girl. Come sit on my lap." Gunnir turned in his chair, his fork still in his hand, and motioned to her.

Each muscle in my body went rigid. She looked at me before stepping toward him and taking a painful seat on his lap. He dug into his food as his hand rested on the small of her back. No one spoke. We just let him eat. He stuffed the chicken into his mouth, only taking his hand off her to rip more meat from the bone. When it was almost picked clean, he held the bone between his greasy fingers and brought it to Ophelia's mouth.

"Suck on it," he said as he rubbed it along her lower lip.

She shook her head.

"If you don't, I'll put my dick in your mouth instead," he cooed, speaking like he was trying to encourage a naughty child to finish the last bite of food on their plate.

Ophelia loosened her lips, and he wiggled the bone into her mouth, groaning as he moved it in and out. When that wasn't enough to satisfy him, he brought his hand to the back of her head and pushed it deeper. As she started to gag, I worried he'd go further and make her blow him. I didn't want to fight my brother again, but I would if he crossed the line. He hadn't yet, but he was inching closer.

"You sure can suck, can't you?" Gunnir asked as he pulled the bone from her mouth. "Now I know why you have Alex so fucking pussy whipped."

"I don't," she whispered, wiping the grease from her chin.

"You do. I've known Alex his entire life, and I never thought I'd walk in on him trying to make a bitch come," Gunnir said with a laugh. He turned toward me. "What were you going to get out of it?"

I had to think fast. "I'd have fucked her after. Have you

been inside them once you make them come? It's even better if you're inside them *when* they come. The way they clench your dick . . ." I gave a convincing groan.

Gunnir's eyes narrowed on me. "You're telling me you've made other bitches come from fucking them?"

"Yeah. They fight the fuck out of it, but that almost makes it feel better." It was true. It happened out of nowhere, usually. I'd fuck them in just the right way, and they would cry harder as they clenched around me. Nothing made me come faster than that surprise orgasm ripping through them. I had gotten close with Ophelia. She'd started to spasm around me and I'd wanted to push her over the edge, but she never got there. Maybe that's why I wanted to bring her there so badly now.

"That ain't never happened to me," Gunnir said.

I laughed. "Not surprised, considering that stubby little dick of yours."

He released Ophelia, and she fell to her back as he jumped to his feet. She landed with a thud and backed herself across the hardwood floors to get away from him.

"What'd you say about my dick?" Gunnir stepped closer, keeping his arms slightly lifted from his sides to make himself look larger.

I stood and stared into his squinted eyes. "It's about the size of that fucking chicken bone," I said with a smirk.

"Fuck you, Alex. Always thinking you're better than me."

Gunnir had lost all interest in Ophelia. I gave her a gentle wave toward the bedroom, and she lifted her chain so it wouldn't make a sound as she slipped away to safety.

Good girl, I thought, before Gunnir came at me with his fist.

I dodged his initial blow, but the second swing connected with the right side of my face. I stumbled back a step, touching my cheek for a moment before I charged at him and knocked him off his feet. My fists pummeled his face until his nose sprayed blood.

"Fuck you, Gunnir. I *am* better than you," I said. I launched a wad of spit to the floor near his head. "You're everything I hated about The Man."

"Get the fuck off me," he growled as he bucked me off him much too easily. "Go kiss your bitch's feet before I fucking kill you!"

I shook out my hand, got up, and walked to my bedroom, locking the door behind me. Ophelia sat on the floor, but she jumped to her feet and came toward me when she heard the lock click. She took my hand in hers and ran her fingers over my bloody knuckles.

"Why?" she asked.

"Why what?"

"Why did you cause a fight like that?"

"He would have done something worse to you."

She shook her head. "Why protect me, though? What good can come from it?"

"Nothing good will come from it, but things are already in motion toward a destination I don't fucking like. So, it is what it is."

She leaned in and kissed me, her chain rattling as she lifted her other hand to my face. My body tensed. She shouldn't have seen me as some white knight. I wasn't. I was fiercely possessive of her. I selfishly wanted to keep her for myself, and I was messing with the household's dynamic to keep a hold on her. I didn't do it because I liked how smart she was or how she was stronger than other girls when she was beneath me. It wasn't because she could wipe the floor with me in checkers or because she seemed to care when I showed her a picture of my mother. It wasn't because she remembered something as stupid as how I liked my eggs.

Fuck. It was all those things.

And it couldn't be any of them.

I stopped her deepening kiss and put distance between us by holding her shoulders. I'd put more distance between us with what I said next. "I don't do what I do because I'm a saint. I do it because I'm a demon disguised as one."

Her lower lip formed a perfect pout, and her eyes lifted to mine. "I don't understand."

"I'm not protecting you. I'm owning you. I'm keeping you from him because I don't want anyone else touching you. I want to be the only one inside you. You can't like me, Ophelia. If he thinks you like me, he'll kill you. If he thinks I like you, he'll kill me. No matter what, you have to be disgusted by me. You have to hate me around him." I drew a sharp inhale. "You have to hate me anyway."

Her lip trembled and her eyes rounded with a sadness I'd never seen. "Oh," she said. She took a step back . . . and then another.

Seeing how my truth broke her made my heart ache, but I had to set these boundaries between us. For both of us. I doubled down. "Did you really think I cared about you?"

Tears welled in her eyes. "No."

She was lying—that word was as plastic as when she pretended to get off—but I was lying too. I cared for her in ways I'd never cared for anyone before. But this house was too small, leaving no room for feelings like that. If Gunnir had lost his mind because I'd tried to get her off, there was no telling how he would react if he knew I was falling for her.

Maybe I didn't have to make her feel completely rejected. I was a Bruggar, after all, and the way she'd come onto me moments before had made me throb. I could put the ball in her court and let her decide. "Don't just stand there like a whipped puppy. If you want something, I'll give it to you, but just be sure you know what this is. If you want something good between the evil here, that's fine, but it's not love or anything."

I expected her to stay back. I could still see the hurt on her face. Instead, she surprised me and walked back into my arms. I didn't kiss her, though. I grabbed her shoulders and pushed her to her knees.

"Show me how you can suck, O," I commanded as I fisted her hair.

She kept silent as I worked down my jeans and pulled out my cock, then her eyes found mine as she wrapped her hand around my dick and stroked me. There was a jagged roughness when I forced someone's hand onto my dick, but Ophelia's touch was soft and smooth, riding from the base to the tip. I'd fucked a lot, but I could count on one hand the times a woman willingly stroked me.

I grabbed the back of her head, but she placed her hand on my wrist.

"Alex, let me do it," she whispered.

Though it went against everything I'd been taught, I let her take control. My hands dropped to my sides, and she opened her mouth and guided me past her waiting lips. My abs tightened as her warm tongue wrapped around me in a way it couldn't when I forced her. It swirled around the head, and I fought the intense urge to grab the back of her head and fuck her face. There was no need to, though. She brought me to the back of her throat.

Willingly.

"Goddamnit, O," I growled. I wrapped my hand within her dark hair without disrupting the movement of her mouth. The way she sucked me felt better than when she fought me, and I didn't want to interrupt this gift she'd given me. I'd never felt such a thing.

It felt too fucking good, though, and I still had plans to make my earlier fantasy a reality. I dragged her onto her feet and kissed her hard. Before she could catch her breath, I led her to the dresser and pushed her chest onto it. I kicked open her legs and her breath hitched, anticipating what she thought would happen next. She had no idea what I wanted to do to her. As much as my dick throbbed to be inside her, I had no plans to force myself on her. Instead, I dropped to my knees.

"Alex," she whimpered.

"What, O?" I asked, blowing a warm breath over her swollen clit.

"I don't know if I want this," she whispered.

"Just hide your moans."

I didn't care what Gunnir thought at that moment. I only wanted to taste her on my tongue. I licked from the swell of her clit to her entrance. I'd never had the urge to go down on a woman, but once I tasted her, it ignited a fire in my belly. She smelled like me. Like the soap we'd used in the shower earlier. She bit into her arm to muffle the whimpers she couldn't control, and her body reacted to each movement of my tongue. I stroked my dick as she grinded on my face from above. I gripped her perfect ass with my other hand and licked at her until her thighs trembled.

"Come for me," I growled against her.

Like a wave, her orgasm swelled and headed for shore. I shoved my fingers inside her and rubbed her clit with my thumb as I licked and nipped at her sensitive, swollen lips. She squeezed around me and clutched the wood, shuddering so hard it made the mirror rattle against the wall. I fucked her with my fingers until she stopped quivering, until her body only jolted with each pass of my thumb over her clit. When I knew she'd ridden out the last of that wave, I stood up, turned her around, and kissed her.

"Clean me up, O," I said against her mouth. She went to lift her hand toward my face, but I pinned it at her side. She understood what I wanted and licked my chin in a long, broad stroke. "Good fucking girl," I growled.

We were heading for the deep end without a life preserver. No one was there to save us, and we were too caught up in each other to save ourselves.

CHAPTER THIRTEEN

OPHELIA

The moment Gunnir caught Alex with his hand between my legs, the air in the house shifted. Even if Gunnir hardly acknowledged what he saw, I felt the hatred radiating from his oily skin. His brooding rage would eventually erupt, and waiting for the impending explosion had set me on edge.

What happened with Alex the night before didn't help my nerves. He confused the hell out of me by making me feel good.

I knew why he'd said what he said about feelings, and he was right. Any feelings would hurt one or both of us. But no matter what lie he tried to tell me, I knew he felt something for me. He wanted to possess me, and no one wanted to own something they didn't like.

Gunnir walked into the bedroom, and my eyes snapped to him. Alex wasn't behind him. My heart fluttered with fear as he unlocked my chain and dragged me into the living room. I tried to dig my heels into the hardwood, but he was too large and powerful. Then I spotted it. There on the floor, with wood remnants curled around the metal edges, was a freshly installed anchor.

"What's happening?" I asked.

"You can't be trusted," Gunnir said as he locked my chain to the loop. "Now you'll be out here so you can't get him into any more trouble."

I sat on the floor and scooted backward until I hit the wall. There was no arguing with Gunnir. I was just stuck, made vulnerable in the middle of the house.

"Where's Alex?"

Gunnir scoffed. "You shouldn't be asking where your fucking master is, girl. You should be glad he's not home and that your pretty little pussy is getting a break."

I struggled to see Alex as a master. He was my captor, but he tried to be good, even if he couldn't because of his evil brother and the horrible man whose presence still haunted the halls of that house.

"Who do you think you are, anyway? We brought you into our home and you try to make Alex like you. For what? So you don't get fucked like the whore you are?" He patted his belly. "Alex is too much of a pussy, but I see what you're doing. You're using him, and it should be the other way around, girl."

I fought the urge to shake my head. Alex wasn't as weak as Gunnir thought. He was strong enough to see that he didn't have to grow up to be quite like the male role models in his life. He just wasn't strong enough to stop the cycle of cruelty. For that, he was weak.

Gunnir went to the kitchen and returned with a bag of rice in his big hand. He shook it, and the uncooked pieces tumbled over each other. He squatted down and poured a thick pile of rice at his feet. Once he'd emptied the bag, he pocketed it in his overalls. He reached for me, and I whimpered as he dragged me to my feet. The moment I stood, he took out the backs of my knees and sent me onto all fours on the mound of uncooked rice. He lifted my chest so I was forced to kneel, and the hard granules burrowed into my skin. The pain was unexpected. I never imagined that such tiny objects could induce such excessive anguish. I cried out and Gunnir smacked my cheek.

"Stay there, girl, or I'll do something worse than make you kneel on some rice." A sadistic smile spread across his face. "Keep your hands in front of you until I tell you to get up. If I see you move, I'll fuck your mouth. Do you understand?"

I nodded, fighting back tears as my knees screamed for relief I couldn't offer them. I didn't do anything to deserve this punishment. I never wanted to be there in the first place. I never asked for any of this, including the pleasure Alex offered. My body responded, even if I didn't want it to. But there was no telling Gunnir that. All he saw was the curl of my hips against his brother's hand.

ALEXZANDER

I CUT the ignition and inhaled a deep breath before going inside. Gunnir had me on eggshells and I hated it. But I wasn't surprised by it. The Man would have killed me if he saw me pleasing one of the girls. It was a foreign and forbidden concept.

I walked inside and nearly dropped the bags of groceries onto the ground. The open door behind me shined sweet sunshine into Ophelia's eyes. She was kneeling, her hands on her thighs. At first I thought that was all it was. Then my eyes registered the stray grains of rice scattered around her. Gunnir had taken a stress position to a new level. When he heard the door close, he came from his room and marched toward me with his head high and his shoulders back.

"What the hell are you doing, Gunnir?" I asked as I put the groceries on the counter and walked toward Ophelia. Pain washed her face, ridding it of color. She looked so obedient. Small and pliable. And I hated that for her. I controlled the tremble of my hands at my sides. I couldn't let Gunnir see how much it angered me.

"She needs to learn her place," he said with a shrug.

Ophelia flinched as she shifted her weight. The Man had taught the rice trick to Gunnir. I never used it because it had been used on me, and I could still recall the pain that raked my whole body, starting in my knees. I didn't wish it on anyone, least of all Ophelia. As I looked down at her, she reminded me of the innocent person I used to be. She reminded me of the person I was before The Man taught me to be more like him.

I needed to get her up, but to do so, I had to keep her down. I walked over and fisted her hair. She whimpered and tensed against my rough grasp.

"Have you learned?" I asked. I forced a sadistic smirk onto my face. She gave me a weak nod, and I gripped her cheeks, sending a breath of surprise past her lips.

I tugged down my zipper and pulled out my cock. She looked up at me with a curled lip, the anger radiating from her as her eyes rolled up my body. I pushed my dick past her tensed mouth. Gunnir kept talking behind me, but I couldn't hear anything over the amplified sound of my heartbeat in my ears. I supported the back of her head to keep her from rocking on her knees as I fucked her mouth. Her lips trembled around my length and her hands pushed at my thighs, but I didn't relent. I couldn't.

"God, I want to feel her mouth, too," Gunnir groaned from the couch. Skin on skin sounded around me as he jerked off to me fucking her face.

"I'm using her," I told him as I pulled the fabric away from her breasts. Exposing her would get him closer. He wouldn't be able to wait for me to finish. I toyed with her nipple between my fingers, and her nails dug into my thigh. I tried to block out the look of betrayal on her face by tilting her head and pushing deeper into her mouth.

Gunnir stood up and stepped closer. My stomach lurched at the sight of him jerking the head of his cock so close to her perfectly pale skin. I thought he just wanted to get a closer look at her body.

I thought wrong.

Gunnir groaned, and his come splashed against her chest. I couldn't finish after seeing his vile jizz painted across her skin. I softened in her mouth, but I kept my hand buried in her hair so I still seemed hard inside her. Then I faked my own orgasm, which left a confused look on her face. I pulled out of her mouth, and she pretended to swallow.

Good girl.

Before Gunnir could do anything more with her, I lifted her off her unsteady knees. Grains of rice released from her skin and clacked onto the floor as she took uneasy steps forward.

"Don't fucking do shit like this without me," I told him as I gestured toward her bleeding knees.

"Don't lose yourself in some fucking pussy, then," he snarled back. Thankfully that was all the fight he had in him, and he waddled toward his room with a satiated sigh.

I helped Ophelia to the bathroom. The moment I closed the door, she swung around to face me with a hard expression written across her face. My eyes dropped to the white pearls of come across her bare chest.

"How could you?" she asked. "Why would you let your disgusting brother—"

I put a hand to her mouth, turned her around, and pulled

her against me. "Shut your mouth," I whispered. "Everything I've allowed is the better of two evils. I've managed to keep him out of your mouth and pussy, have I not?" I leaned closer to her ear. "Would you have preferred it if I stepped back and let him come on your tongue instead of your chest?"

Ophelia whimpered and shook her head in understanding. I released her mouth. She reached down and picked at the rice that had wormed into her skin. "Fuck, that hurt," she said.

"He did it because he thinks I like you, didn't he?"

She nodded. "He thinks I'm getting to you."

I looked away from her.

She *was* getting to me, and I didn't know how to stop it. I'd never felt this way toward anyone, let alone a captive. She was meant to be a doll on a chain, something to use and play with whenever I saw fit, but she'd never been that to me. Not even when I'd used her in the beginning. Ophelia felt more like a gift. Her body was something to cherish, and I wanted to fucking cherish her. Which was why this situation was driving me mad.

I grabbed a rag from under the sink and ran it beneath the tap. I wiped at her skin, fighting the gag and the curl of my lip over the trail of shiny residue running down her chest. She kept staring up at me, something unreadable filtering through her eyes as I cleaned her. I pulled her into me. I didn't care that Gunnir's remnants still coated her skin or that I could smell him on her. Despite all of it, I still felt a draw toward her mouth, where her lips were still puffy from my cock.

I let myself be weak. I leaned into her for a kiss, and she welcomed me.

My hands went to her buttons. I fastened them, concealing her vulnerable chest. I placed my hands around her waist and lifted her onto the counter so I could tend to her knees. She flinched as I grazed her raw skin with my fingertips. Each grain had either left a tiny impression or ripped her flesh.

Pockets of blood filled the miniature channels. Touching her knees reminded me of when I'd been forced to kneel on a bed of rice for almost a full twenty-four hours. If she looked close enough, she'd see the scars on my knees.

Kneeling on rice was bad enough, but having to do it while your skin was still raw was worse. So much worse.

"I'm sorry," I said as I held the cool rag to her knees. "You deserve better than this."

Her eyes met mine. "Then let me go," she whispered.

That hurt. It shouldn't have, because they all wanted to escape, but I expected her to want to stay with me.

I brushed a hand down her cheek. "I can't." I shook my head. "I won't let you go."

"If you care about me at all—"

"Don't, Ophelia. I can't let you go because I'll lose the parts of me I found inside you."

Tears glossed her eyes. "You could come with me."

I tended to her knees and ignored her suggestion. There was nothing more for me to say. I couldn't let her go. Logistically, it would have been fucking dumb. She'd only realize how stupid she'd been to fall for me, then she'd run to the police. Emotionally? I couldn't lose her. I didn't want to be without her, and leaving together wasn't possible. As much as I despised who my brother had become, he was still my brother. If I could keep Ophelia safe from him here, we could learn to coexist.

I helped her off the counter, and she wobbled to the bedroom on unsteady legs. I closed and locked the door behind us before stripping down to my boxers. The chain clicked as I fastened it to the hook, and like an obedient pet, she went to her corner and began fussing with her thin blankets.

That hard floor will be hell on her knees.

I slipped under the bedcovers and motioned her over, but

she shook her head and remained planted where she sat. I lifted the blanket away. "Come on, O." I wanted her to be comfortable after feeling so much pain.

When she continued to refuse, I went toward her and lifted her from the floor. She was so small within my arms. So fragile and helpless. As I placed her tense body beneath the covers, she looked up at the ceiling and gritted her teeth. She probably worried I'd fuck her now that she was in my bed, but I didn't force my touch. I slipped one hand behind my head and kept the other on my bare stomach.

The evening crawled into nighttime, and her rigid muscles began to relax. A long exhale left her chest, and I knew she missed sleeping in a bed. Who wouldn't? The floor was a cold and lonely place.

Just before I fell asleep, she turned toward me, draped her arm over my waist, and nestled into me. I wrapped my arm around her. This foreign action felt so forbidden, like I'd be punished for offering and finding comfort against her skin. I'd been taught that Bruggars didn't need affection, and women didn't deserve it. But I didn't care anymore. I basked in her warmth. She felt so good in my arms, like she belonged.

But we both knew she didn't.

CHAPTER FOURTEEN

OPHELIA

I woke up in Alex's embrace sometime before sunrise. I tried not to rattle my chain as I turned my head and realized how I'd fallen asleep. He snored beside me, and we were both in his bed. One of his arms circled me, and mine curled around his waist. It would have felt like we were a couple waking up after a passionate night together . . . if it hadn't been for the chain weighing down my neck. The rub of metal reminded me I was his captive. That I was in bed, *cuddling* with my captor.

When I tried to peel away from him, he stirred awake. His eyes opened, heavy with sleep, and as he stretched, I spotted the hard length tenting his boxers. He noticed my open staring and covered his crotch with the sheet.

"Morning," he whispered. It felt and sounded too normal. His hand grazed my side, leaving goosebumps behind. Part of me wanted to spit fire at him and tell him not to touch me. Another part of me reveled in the way his fingertips whispered over my skin. It was kind, almost loving.

It was also wrong. So fucking wrong.

I pulled away and sat up without responding, but he pushed me down with a stern grasp on my shoulder. "What's the matter?" he asked, his green eyes dark and intense.

"We can't cuddle like this," I told him as I once more tried to get up.

"I wasn't the one who cuddled up to you, O," he said as he pulled me closer and kissed me.

I pushed at his chest. "No," I whispered as his lips ran along my jaw.

"I want you," he growled.

I looked at the ceiling, mentally preparing to disappear within my head as he took me. When he didn't climb over me, I blinked away the dread but refused to look at him.

Alex grabbed my chin and turned my face toward him. "I don't want you to go somewhere else in your head." He smirked, his fingers grazing my jaw. "It doesn't have to be what it's been."

He leaned in and kissed my chest. My stomach tightened as I remembered Gunnir's come marking that same spot, but Alex didn't seem to care as he devoured me. His fingers worked open my buttons and his mouth captured my nipple. I wanted to stop him because he didn't deserve to kiss me. He said we couldn't have feelings, he'd reiterated how fatal they'd be, and yet there he was, acting like I was more than just his captive.

His hand moved down to my stomach, and I caught it before he went any lower. "You're putting a lot on me that you shouldn't. You're telling me to enjoy this, but I can't enjoy this hell."

Alex brushed the hair from my cheek. "I know we're in hell, but it doesn't have to be all fire and brimstone. It doesn't always have to burn."

"Maybe it's not burning you, Alex, but I'm on fire."

He rested his chin on my chest. "I can't give you heaven, but I can make hell feel good sometimes."

"That sounds like a devil's bargain."

"Maybe," he said as he spread my shirt and trailed kisses down my stomach. "But the devil doesn't bargain."

"What if I say no, Alex? Will you take it anyway?"

He stopped his descent and brought his face to mine. I felt every ounce of his strength as he hovered over me, and the hard heat pressing between us was a threat I'd felt too many times already.

A frustrated breath eased from his lips and rolled over me, and his eyes met mine. "As much as I want to sink inside you again, I'll stop. For you."

I exhaled my relief.

"That doesn't mean you're off the hook. Patience is a virtue, but I'm not a virtuous man." His eyes flashed with an idea, and a sly smile spread his lips. "Play checkers with me."

ALEXZANDER

I WAS BEING A CERTIFIABLE CREEP, but did I care? Not a bit. I didn't take her mouth or her pussy, but I needed to come, and I wanted to be slaughtered by her in checkers while I did. She always thought out every move, and the way she bit her lip when she focused drove me nuts.

"Get the game," I told her. "But keep your shirt unbuttoned for me."

She got out of bed and pulled the box from the closet. She kept her gaze on the floor as she sat across from me and prepared the board. The two pieces of aged cardboard didn't want to lie flat on the lumpy mattress, but she fiddled with it until she made it work. My eyes went to her soft hands. She fondled each piece near her breasts before leaning over to place them down. I imagined putting my dick between those breasts. Every part of her was so fuckable.

I pulled my cock through the slit in my boxers and stroked myself as we played. Just like I'd hoped, she leaned over, bit her lip, and examined every move. Her competitive need to win helped her ignore the fact that I was jerking off as she played out each move. She was wiping the floor with me, and her pride made me stroke myself faster.

Just as she finished her final move, as her tits pressed together when she leaned over, as her dark hair grazed her pale skin, I came. I caught most of it in my hand, but some squirted across the board. Her eyes rushed to mine because we both knew who would be cleaning up that mess.

"Get on your knees and get it up, O," I said through a groan.

Her mouth gaped. "Really?"

I nodded, but she didn't move. That was probably because her knees still hurt, but it wasn't like I was making her kneel on the ground. I wiped my hand on an old shirt, stood up, and knocked her forward. With both hands, I brushed her hair away from her face and gripped it behind her head. When I pushed her head down, she put out her tongue and obediently licked up my come. She curled her lip in disgust, but I fucking loved it. I hated seeing her obedience when Gunnir issued commands, but I loved seeing glimpses of that for me.

She continued to lap up my come. With the chain extending from the loop around her neck, she looked like a dog. A sudden pang of guilt squeezed my chest. She was too beautiful to be a dog.

"O," I whispered, and lifted her by her hair. A drop of come dangled from her lower lip, and I leaned down and took the salty taste of myself into my mouth. I kissed her, transferring more of my remnants from her tongue to mine. She welcomed me into her mouth, and I growled. If she was gonna be a dog, I'd join her pack.

My eyes caught on the door, and I pulled away from her. The lock was no longer engaged, but I was certain I'd locked it when we came in last night. Because of her chain, there was no way Ophelia could have reached the door. Which only meant one thing.

CHAPTER FIFTEEN

OPHELIA

We stayed in bed all day, dreading the confrontation that would surely arise. We played a few games of checkers, but mostly we just sat in silence. We couldn't stay holed up in that room forever, though, and Alex finally went to feel things out when early evening set in.

Minutes passed like hours as I sat on the mattress and listened for the argument to begin, but instead of shouting and destruction, I only heard birds twittering outside the window. When he returned, he had a puzzled look on his face.

"He's not here," he said, running his hand through his hair.

"Where would he go? Is he in the basement with Sam?"

He shook his head. "No, the door's still bolted shut. I have no idea."

As if to end our confusion, the front door slammed and heavy footsteps stomped through the front of the house. Moments later, the sound of clanging pans was followed by the scent of burning food.

"Is he cooking?" I asked.

"I don't think he knows how to cook. We'd better get out there and see what's up. Maybe he has Sam in the kitchen."

He dressed me and made sure I was buttoned to the top to avoid drawing Gunnir's attention when we left the room. The moment we stepped into the kitchen, Gunnir shot us a merry greeting.

"Glad you two could finally join me," he said as he piled burned eggs onto a couple of plates.

Alex and I exchanged a quick glance before I turned my attention to the charred globs and wished I'd been commanded to cook the breakfast. At least it would have been palatable.

"Have a seat, girl," Gunnir said as he gestured toward a chair with the spatula.

The hair on my neck stood on end. He never allowed me to eat with them, let alone take a seat at the table. I needed to obey, however, so I did as I was told and sat in the chair he'd chosen. My eyes flitted around the room, searching for a sign of the plan he had up his sleeve.

Eggshells littered the counter, and a haze of smoke hung in the air. A black mess coated the pan he'd used to char the eggs, and it would take a week's worth of elbow grease to get it clean again. Gunnir walked over and threw a plate of dark, sticky eggs in front of me. My eyes rolled up his body, lingering on the unclipped strap slapping against his belly as he stepped back. I tried to avoid looking at his hideous face, but I was drawn up to his mouth. It tilted at the corners in an uneven, sadistic smile. He reached over and nudged the fork toward me.

I lifted the food to my mouth and tried to hold back a grimace when charcoal coated my tongue. After reminding myself to be grateful, I swallowed. This was probably more than Sam had gotten all day. If she got anything at all.

Alex ate as much of the noxious eggs as he could, but Gunnir didn't dig in with his usual gusto. Instead, he picked around his plate and kept glancing at Alex. I worried the eggs might have been poisoned. It would have been an easy way to cut me from the equation. Then again, I didn't really care to be part of their fucked-up math problem, so I kept eating.

The mumble of fuzzy daytime television drifted from the living room, but the meal was otherwise silent. When Alex finished eating, Gunnir finally spoke.

"Got a deer this afternoon," he said to Alex. "I need you to dress it so we can get the meat in the freezer before it spoils."

Alex lowered his fork and glanced at me.

"Quit worrying about her," Gunnir said with a grin. "I swear on the Bruggar name that I won't lay a hand on her. Just dress the fucking deer so we can feed ourselves. It's out back, close to the bend in the creek. Can't miss it."

Alex slid the chair away from the table and got to his feet. "You didn't bother dragging it closer to the house?" He shook his head. "Of course you didn't," he mumbled.

I didn't like where this was going, but Alex didn't seem too worried. Gunnir said he wouldn't lay a hand on me, and that left no room for argument as far as he was concerned. If I tried to argue, it would only show Gunnir how much I trusted Alex, and that would be bad for both of us.

Alex put on a jacket and went to the door, daring to look at me one more time before leaving the house. I pleaded with my eyes. Without words, I begged him to find some reason to stay.

But he left.

Gunnir went to the kitchen window and watched until Alex's figure disappeared into the trees. "This will do," he said as he pulled something from behind the fridge and pointed it toward me; it was a long rod with two points at the end. "I said I wouldn't lay a hand on you, but I don't need hands to make you move. Get up." He pressed a button, and a loud clicking sound erupted from the points, jumping together in a bright arc of electricity.

I looked out the window and considered screaming for Alex. He wasn't too far off, but Gunnir's weapon was closer. Instead of calling for help, I stood on shaking legs and waited for my next command.

Gunnir motioned toward the hall, talking as we walked. "You like sleeping with Alex in a nice comfy bed, huh? Spoiled girl."

I shook my head.

"Sure you do. I saw you two, all curled up in each other's arms. It was so dang sweet." Gunnir snatched my chain, bringing me to a halt in front of the bathroom as his smile morphed into a frown. "I'll show you a nice little bed, girl. Get in the tub."

I swallowed. "I don't understand," I whispered as I stepped into the bath. I was so fucking confused.

He gripped the chain and snatched me into a sitting position. "Unbutton your shirt," he whispered as he squatted beside the tub. When I didn't, he brought the tip of the cattle prod into view. Fear overtook my nervous system, and my hands hurried to unfasten each button until I'd fully exposed myself. Gunnir groaned at the sight of my chest. "Shrug outta it. I don't want it getting all wet."

Wet?

I removed my shirt and drew my knees to my chest to hide my breasts.

"Boxers too," Gunnir said as he motioned to the underwear concealing what I desperately wanted to keep hidden. I slipped them off and pulled my knees to my chest once more, but my legs could only cover so much.

Gunnir undid his remaining strap, and his overalls fell and bunched at his knees. He stood beside me, his belly hanging past his dingy white underwear. His hand went for his small, limp cock, and another bolt of fear tore through me. I was too scared to move, so I dropped my gaze and tried to ignore the hardening dick beside my head. I waited for him to grab me and put himself in my mouth, and my stomach lurched with disgust at the impending intrusion. Alex couldn't save me this time.

Warm liquid splashed my skin, focusing on my chest, and a pungent scent filled my nose. The stream moved toward my head, soaking my hair in a waterfall of urine. My stomach climbed into my throat and up came the eggs, which tasted worse the second time around. Warm piss and chunks of vomit coated my chest and collected between my legs. I couldn't even open my mouth to cry out because if I did, his piss would worm its way onto my tongue. I could only cover my head with my arms to protect my eyes and nose. I called to Alex in my mind, wishing he hadn't left me, begging him to save me.

Please . . .

ALEXZANDER

I'D INTENTIONALLY "FORGOTTEN" my hunting knife in a drawer in the kitchen so I had a reason to return, but I still had to make it believable. Gunnir needed to think I'd gotten all the way to the deer carcass before realizing I'd left it behind. I waited at the edge of the woods, listening for a scream or a scuffle inside the house, but the silence was more unnerving than a shout for help. Adrenaline built up in my muscles until I had to move. I had to know she was safe from him.

I ran toward the house and steadied my breathing as I

opened the front door. They weren't in the living room or the kitchen, and the basement door was still bolted shut. I stopped and listened. Odd sounds drifted from the hall, and when I turned the corner, I saw what was causing the noise. Gunnir's overalls were around his knees, and he was pissing into the bathtub. He groaned, a hand on his hip as the stream sputtered out and ended. Only once he took a step back did I see Ophelia, naked and curled into a terrified ball. She was soaked.

"What the fuck?" I asked. It was all I could think to say.

Gunnir held his hand toward Ophelia, showcasing his handiwork as if he'd just painted a masterpiece with his dick. "Just showing the girl here what kind of bed she deserves."

So I'd been right. He'd seen us asleep in the bed.

Gunnir put his arm around my shoulder and reached toward my fly. I knocked his hand away and lost my footing on the slick floor, but his grasp on my neck kept me on my feet. His hand reached for my fly again, but I shook my head.

"Piss on her," Gunnir snarled.

My head never stopped shaking. Not until he pulled the cattle prod from behind the toilet. For being as big and stupid as he was, he wasn't a complete moron. He was intelligent as hell when it came to torture.

I didn't care. I'd take the prod. I refused to piss on her.

Instead of turning the weapon toward me, the humming crackle moved toward Ophelia. She screamed, her body trembling as the prod inched closer to her bare skin. Her eyes snapped to mine.

"Fine!" I said, just before the prongs reached her. "I'll fucking do it."

"Atta boy," Gunnir said, clapping a hand against my back.

I opened my fly, unable to look at her through the veil of guilt hanging over me. With my eyes aimed at the ceiling, I began to piss. My stream connected with ceramic and flesh, and she let out a weak whimper. That sound broke me; it would have taken me off my feet had Gunnir not been holding me up. Once I finished, he let me go and I fell to my knees.

"A pussy and his whore," Gunnir snarled as he pulled up his overalls and left us alone in the bathroom.

The door slammed and I tried to gather the strength to sit up. Ophelia was sobbing, and the smell of urine hung in the air like a nightmarish perfume.

"I'm so fucking sorry," I whispered, but she didn't acknowledge me. Her eyes told me everything I needed to know, though. That she was right. That she was in hell and no matter how much I tried to shield her from the heat, I couldn't stop the encroaching firestorm. And now the flames were burning me too.

Ophelia went silent, which was worse than her crying. She sat there, bathed in the devil's piss, unable to move. Fighting through the adrenaline crash, I gathered enough strength to reach up and turn on the shower. The water fell from the showerhead, spraying us both, and her chest drew in with a sharp gasp as the cold water struck her and soaked her hair. Without getting undressed, I climbed into the tub and helped her to her feet, but she was deadweight in my hands.

"Ophelia, come on," I said in a strained voice. I finally got her onto her feet and pushed the hair from her face. "Oh god," I whispered as I looked into eyes so full of mistrust. My participation had destroyed her, and that gutted me.

Ignoring the heaviness in my arms, I washed her off. She leaned into me as I scrubbed her hair until the floral scent overtook the urine. Once she was clean, I helped her out of the shower, wrapped a towel around her, and brought her to my room. I locked the door and pulled the dresser in front of it.

I stripped the wet clothes from my body and dressed in something dry, and when I turned around, I found her shivering and staring at me. I lifted the blanket on the bed, urging her to disappear into its warmth, but she wouldn't move. She was scared of me again. Afraid of what I would do to her once I climbed in beside her. I grabbed her arm, eased her onto the bed, and pulled the blanket over her naked body. Her eyes never left me, anticipating what she feared would happen next. Instead of crawling in beside her, I locked her chain to the anchor and curled up on the floor. I pulled the thin blanket over me and found comfort in its scent. It smelled like her.

I didn't know why I was so bothered by what happened. Gunnir and I had done worse than that to nearly all the women. We used to make them drink our piss before bed so they'd taste us all night. Ophelia was different, though. Seeing that defeated look on her face reminded me too much of what Gunnir and The Man had done to me. Before my eyes, she became that traumatized little boy tied to the post outside because he snuck his mother some extra food. Ophelia was the good part of me, the part that was beaten into oblivion, leaving just the monster in my skin.

Lulled by the hum of the radiator beside me, I let myself slip into sleep. Gunnir would kill me if he knew I gave her my bed, but I was the one who deserved to sleep on the fucking floor.

How would she ever forgive me? How could I forgive myself?

Chapter Sixteen

Ophelia

Waking up the next morning meant I was still trapped in the nightmare I fell asleep in. What happened last night was . . . I couldn't even let myself get lost in that memory again. When I turned over and looked out the window, it was still dark outside. There was a moment of panic when I realized I was alone in the bed, but Alex's snores from the floor gave me a moment of comfort. I didn't remember very much after they pissed on me. I remembered things like the way Gunnir's jaw hung loose from the pleasure of what he was doing, or the way Alex hadn't wanted to participate. I hardly remembered the shower or Alex cleaning me up, but the familiar scent of cheap soap comforted me further.

My chain rattled and slid against his foot as I tried to climb out of bed.

"O?" he whispered, his voice heavy with sleep.

"It's me," I said as I scooted against the headboard.

I didn't expect him to clamber to his feet and rush to comfort me. I didn't want his comfort. He was one half of the two-part golden shower I received. Regardless of what I wanted, he came toward me and wrapped his arms around my shoulders. "I'm so fucking sorry," he whispered. Even in the darkness, I knew there was hurt in his expression. I could hear it in his voice, which was fine, because he deserved to feel as terrible as I did. "I had to do it. He would have shocked you with that fucking prod if I hadn't."

"I'd have preferred that," I said.

"He would have prodded your . . ." Alex couldn't finish the sentence, as if locked in a violent memory. "Trust me, you wouldn't have preferred it," he finally said.

"Why don't you stand up to him? If not for me, at least do it for yourself." I leaned away from his touch.

"You wouldn't understand," he said with a small shake of his head.

I was surprised he couldn't feel the heat of my stare through the darkness. "Pathetic," I said with a scoff.

I shouldn't have said it, but the word leapt from my throat and landed on him before I knew what was happening. I saw how much he disliked his brother and fought against the way he ran things, but he did *nothing* to change it. He merely danced around Gunnir's sick desires to try to spare me the worst of it. I wasn't unappreciative, but he hadn't been kidding when he said he wasn't a white knight. He was a demon fighting the hold of the devil, steering his flames in other directions. He *couldn't* save me. No matter how hard he tried, the devil still found ways to set me alight.

Instead of making me pay for calling him pathetic, he spoke to me through gritted teeth, showing restraint that must have been difficult for him. "Don't talk to me like that."

"Or what? You'll kill me?" I said. Again, I knew I shouldn't have continued to goad him, but after what happened last night, I wasn't keen on continuing this life, day in and day out. I was already so fucking tired. If death was the only exit out of that place, so be it.

He didn't respond, so I kept pushing.

"You're stronger than him. You could take him out," I whispered. Physically, Alex didn't have much of a chance, but intellectually, he ran dizzying circles around him. Emotionally, he was more evolved. There were ways to beat the physical differences. We both knew it, even if he didn't want to admit it.

Instead of answering my plea, he wrapped his hand around the back of my head, fisted my hair, and brought his lips to mine in the dark. The wild heat of anger radiated from him, pulling the air from my lungs with a kiss so hard I couldn't even take a breath that wasn't one of his. There was no way to even utter the word *no*. He didn't want to talk anymore, but I needed to. My hands gripped his shirt as I tried to push him away, but he only ripped away the blanket I still clutched against my bare chest.

I whimpered as he laid me down and got between my legs. I didn't want him like this. I wanted to get inside his head.

No, I had gotten into his mind, but that wasn't enough. I had to get into his heart if I had any chance of surviving this. I had to take up more space and overpower the familial bond he shared with his brother.

I opened my mouth to speak, but he pressed his lips to mine again, silencing me. My voice was my only weapon against him, and his defenses were primed to keep me from breaking through.

I put my hands to his face and held him in my hot grasp. "Talk to me, Alex," I whispered.

"Not now, O," he said, lowering his mouth to my chest.

"What are you afraid of?"

"I'm not afraid of Gunnir, if that's what you think," he snapped.

"I'm not talking about Gunnir."

Alex rolled off me and released a deep sigh. "For being as fucking pretty as you are, you sure can kill a moment."

I scoffed. "*This* kills the moment? Out of everything—"

"Ophelia."

"Well, tell me. What are you afraid of?"

Alexzander

WHAT A FUCKING QUESTION. I didn't fear Gunnir, but he was a carbon-copy of the thing I feared most: The Man. He was dead, rendered to nothing but bones along with all the women that crossed this threshold and never left alive, but he still had such a hold on everyone in the home. Even the shadows that walked along the walls were chained to this place from the fear and pain he'd caused. The Man was the maestro, and we were the orchestra that made the music he wanted to hear. Instead of instruments, we played women. The screams, the whimpers, the cries—it was his symphony. Even now, if I tried to stop the solemn tune, my life would end. If Gunnir didn't take my life, he would rip apart the thing I cherished most in the world.

Ophelia.

That's when I realized The Man wasn't what I feared most. I feared love.

If I loved someone, they were ripped from me. They say it's better to have loved and lost than never to have loved at all, but fuck that saying. Whoever came up with it didn't know the true meaning behind it. They didn't grasp the agonizing ache that came with loss. I knew what it meant to lose someone I loved, and it broke me. I vowed I'd never let *anything* or *anyone* into my heart again. Love wasn't something wonderful and powerful. It was more like a disease that plagued my body until I became too weak to live. Love killed the bright parts within me, and I was trying so goddamn hard to keep Ophelia out of the darkness that occupied my heart. I couldn't love her, because then she would be ripped away too.

"What are *you* afraid of?" I asked, because I had no answer for her.

"My father," she said without hesitation. "Even when he'd drift into an alcohol coma, I still couldn't shake the fear I felt with every breath I drew in that house."

I felt that. I really fucking felt that. "What'd he do?"

"Don't ask me that," she said, her voice so low I nearly didn't hear her.

"You can't ask about fears and then close up when asked about yours."

"You weren't exactly forthcoming yourself." She was silent for so long, with nothing but a ticking clock counting the time to interrupt the quiet. Finally, she drew a quivering breath. "He touches me in ways no father should. At first I thought he was too drunk to realize I wasn't my mother, but I later realized he was just sick."

What was left of my heart sank into my belly. "How old were you when it started?"

"I can't remember a time when it wasn't happening."

No wonder she was a fucking pro at disappearing in her mind. She'd had a lifetime of practice.

After another wavering breath, she continued. "Every conscious memory of my father was hell, and it wasn't just because of what he did to me. It was everything. It was his mere existence."

God, I felt that too. A tear forced its way from my eye and

slid toward my ear. No wonder I saw so much of me within her.

She *was* me.

And I had been hellbent on destroying anything good left within her, just like The fucking Man. Just like her father.

I turned my face toward the wall as if she were a bright light that would blind me if I didn't look away. It was too close. *She* was too close. I was fighting to keep her out of my heart, but she was clawing her way inside as a reflection of me stared through the fucking cracks she'd created.

Guilt assaulted me, weighing me down like a monster on my chest, ripping through me to get at the soft parts inside. I was no better than the man she feared most. She was so dead to being forced because that was her home. And forcing myself on her had been mine. We had to move out of that place. We had to leave home, somehow, for good.

"Ophelia," I whispered. "I'm afraid of *you*."

She sat up on her elbows and even in the dark, I sensed the confused glare on her face. Even in the weak moonlight, even with my eyes closed, I could see the crease between her eyebrows. It would be difficult to explain. I wasn't afraid of her physically, but I feared what I could be beneath her. How could she drag me from the depths of hell without leaving herself with mortal wounds?

"I don't understand," she said. "What have I ever done to make you fear me?"

"You're shaking up everything I've ever known. Tearing apart decades of conditioning. It's fucking terrifying. Feeling things is worse than feeling nothing at all."

The mattress sank as she settled beside me again. She was quiet for a while and I began to think she'd grown tired of the conversation, but she'd only been considering what she said next. "I disagree. If we become numb to everything, we lose our humanity. We're reduced to something small and insignificant."

"What do you see me as, O? A predator? The devil? What?"

The bed creaked beneath her as she turned on her side to face me. "At first I saw you as a villain, but I've come to realize you're actually a victim of circumstance."

I scoffed. "Bullshit."

"Not bullshit. Would you do what you've done if you weren't in this house?"

Well, shit. It was hard to tell. I never thought anything was wrong until The Man brought me to the hardware store and I saw women walking around without chains attached to their necks or ankles. There were smiles on their faces. They seemed happy. When I asked him why the women at home needed chains, he told me it was to keep them from running off. My mother kept telling me to stop asking questions, but I couldn't stop, even when The Man beat me for it. Eventually he silenced me.

Even if he quieted my voice, my mind continued to obsess over the foreign ways other people lived. I was like one of those sad bears in the depressing cages at the zoo, never realizing my way of life was unnatural until I saw how bears lived in the wild. Never recognizing that everything around me was a lie. Yet just like a bear in a cage, I wasn't equipped to survive in a natural habitat. There was safety behind these bars. But would I have been able to survive had I not been caged to begin with?

I would never be Gunnir or The Man, that much I knew, but would my dick twitch when a woman fought my touch if I hadn't been trained by Satan himself? It felt so normal. It was how I imagined people felt when they heard someone scream for help, but instead of rushing to their rescue, I felt the urge to hurt them worse. What did that psych student teach me? Nature versus nurture? Could the way I was raised truly suffocate who I might have been?

I didn't know. I would never know.

"I can't answer that," I said.

Her fingers ran along my skin, finding my scars in the dark. "You wouldn't have all these marks on you if that's truly who you were. They wouldn't have had to beat you into this life."

I opened my mouth to argue, but she was right. Did she know what I'd endured? I grabbed her wrist and guided her hand to my knees. "The scars here are from the rice." I gripped her chain and gave it a rattle. "This was my chain before it was yours."

The clouds in the dark sky broke and sent a shaft of moonlight across her face, illuminating the pout of her lower lip and the tear sliding down her cheek.

"None of this excuses what I became," I said. "I'm sure I had a choice somewhere along the line, even if I can't remember one." I sat up at the edge of the bed, and her hand lingered a moment too long on my skin. I went back to the floor and wrapped myself in the blanket so I could try to go back to sleep.

Ophelia's chain rattled as she turned over. "Think what you want, Alex, but I don't believe you'd be holding women captive if it wasn't for Gunnir."

Even if she was right, we couldn't go back in time and rewrite the past. Like the stir-crazy bears in their tiny cages, we could only be what we were.

CHAPTER SEVENTEEN

OPHELIA

I tossed and turned until the sun came up. After our conversation in the dark morning hours, I *almost* asked Alex to stay in bed with me. I longed for the comfort of his heat beside me, but I let him go. He'd seemed so lost in his head, traveling through whatever memories I'd drummed up from his childhood. He was in a constant state of turmoil, torn between the good part of himself and all the bad that had been beaten into him.

When I got up, he was still fast asleep, curled up on himself beneath the blanket that had been my only comfort on that floor. I held my chain to stop it from rattling and waking him. I hadn't heard Gunnir stirring around the house, and I worried the whole nail incident—coupled with the recent issues—had gotten Sam killed. I'd never forgive myself. I was so caught up in trying to escape the basement that I hadn't considered how my actions might have affected her.

I wrapped the blanket around my naked body and slipped my feet to the floor, my gaze shifting between the closet and the dresser against the bedroom door. It would have been easy to grab the gun and take out Alex, then Gunnir when he came into the room. My legs shook, but I took a step toward the closet. I could free myself and get help for Sam. I could end this awful—

I looked down at a peacefully sleeping Alex and found myself glued to the floor. The soft morning light caught in his hair and curved along his strong jaw. His lips—the same lips that had pressed against mine just hours earlier—parted slightly each time he breathed. He didn't look like the man who forced himself on me. He looked like the man who protected me.

I couldn't do it. As bad as my situation was, I couldn't bear the thought of taking his life before he had the chance to learn who he really was. I turned toward the bedroom door. There had to be another way.

"Ophelia?" His sleep-laced voice froze me in place. He reached over and flipped on a lamp sitting on the table beside the bed. "What's going on?"

"I heard a noise," I whispered.

Alex sat up and his posture stiffened. "Gunnir?"

"I don't know." I shook my head. I'd heard absolutely nothing, but I couldn't tell him I had just talked myself out of blowing his head off.

Alex unlocked my chain, got to his feet, and pulled the dresser away from the door. Before his hand reached the knob, his eyes rolled down my blanket-wrapped body. My current attire would send Gunnir into a rabid frenzy, so he dug through the drawer and handed me another pair of boxers and a t-shirt. He opened the door, peered out, then gestured toward the bathroom. I ran to the toilet and tugged down the boxers so I could pee. Gone were the days of caring that Alex was so close when I relieved myself. I'd been holding it for hours. Instead of staring at me, Alex looked at the porcelain sink. My eyes fell to the bathtub, but I shook my head, refusing to relive the piss-filled memory for even a second.

I got up and stepped around him to wash my hands. He went to the toilet, and the sound of his stream colliding with the water sent me back to the bathtub once more. When he finished, he didn't look at me. He was fighting to escape that memory too.

We walked into the kitchen to the sound of a bird singing its morning song near the window. Gunnir's cooking mess still covered the counters. Without being asked, I started to clean up. Like it or not, that hellhole was still my current residence, and I didn't want to live in a pigsty.

Gunnir's heavy footsteps approached from the hall, and my hand stopped its circular motion against the pan in my hand. I tried to steady myself, but every part of me trembled. I heard a second set of footsteps, and I focused my eyes ahead, too afraid to turn around.

"I want to play a game," Gunnir said with a rattle of the chain in his hand.

Sam? If she'd been brought from Gunnir's bedroom, she would have been in the epicenter of hell. She'd have been an arm's length away from the painful grasp of the devil himself. I turned around and looked at her. Black and blue splotches discolored the skin around her eyes, and if I'd ever thought she couldn't lose any more weight, I'd been mistaken. Her tongue tried to wet her cracked lips, but it did no good.

I tried to get her attention, but she wouldn't meet my gaze. I swallowed and let go of the sponge. No one spoke, and Gunnir didn't elaborate on what kind of game he had in mind. The look on Alex's face told me it would not be a fun one.

"Is no one going to ask me what I want to play?" Gunnir prodded.

"Not in the mood, Gunnir," Alex said, crossing his arms over his chest.

Gunnir's sadistic grin said he didn't care if anyone else wanted to play. He wanted to, and that was all that mattered. He walked to the cupboards, dragging Sam along with him, and pulled two saucers from the bottom shelf. Gripping the chain in his fist, he led Sam to the table and placed the saucers beside each other in front of two chairs. "How about a friendly little eating contest?"

Alex cocked his head. "Depends on what we're eating."

"We're not. They are," Gunnir said, gesturing between Sam and me.

Oh god, I thought as I tried to take a step back, but there was nowhere to go. Gunnir grabbed my chain, dragged Sam and me to the hook on the floor, and locked us in place. He gestured for us to drop to our knees, and we obeyed.

Gunnir pulled Alex away from us, and I turned to Sam. "I'm sorry," I said. "I didn't think it through."

"Don't, Ophelia. I would have done the same thing," she whispered before shaking her head.

My eyes were drawn to movement. Alex and Gunnir were locked in a quiet argument. Gunnir pointed an emphatic finger toward us every so often, but I couldn't hear the words slipping past their moving lips. Gunnir motioned to his lap and then pointed at me. Alex shook his head. I didn't need an interpreter for that one. By the time they separated, my stomach was in knots.

Gunnir exited the house through the back door, and Alex gripped one of the saucers in his hand and stepped toward me. He kneeled and looked behind him before leaning into me. "You're not going to like this, but it's better than the original idea."

I closed my eyes. "What am I in for?"

"It's an eating contest, like he said. Whoever cleans their plate first—"

My eyes narrowed. "What are we cleaning off the plate?"

Alex's gaze fell. "Come."

"What?" I said, much too loud.

"Lower your voice, Ophelia." His lips tightened. "Remember what I've told you. Everything I do is to try to get you the better deal. Gunnir wanted us to swap, but I don't want you taking Gunnir's come. You'll get mine."

I shrugged my shoulders and sighed. "Well, that isn't too bad. I've swallowed your come before, so it's not anything new."

He looked like he wanted to kiss me, but he stopped himself. If Gunnir saw something like that, he'd change the rules of the game.

"What happens if I lose?" I asked.

He leaned forward and put his forehead against mine. "Don't."

ALEXZANDER

"READY TO PLAY!" Gunnir screamed as he closed the back door.

I pulled away from Ophelia, wiping my hands on my pants as I sat up. When I turned around, my stomach tightened. Gunnir held a branding iron in his right hand. I didn't want Ophelia to be a player in this game, but I'd given her the best chance at winning. If she'd been forced to eat Gunnir's come, she wouldn't have stood a chance.

Gunnir grabbed the other saucer and knelt in front of the girls with a heavy thud. He placed the saucer in front of him and unclipped his overalls. He pulled his cock from his underwear and tugged at it as he stared at Ophelia.

It would be hard to come with the risk of Ophelia getting branded hanging over me, but I unzipped my pants and pulled out my cock anyway. I had to try. With the way Ophelia looked up at me, though, I couldn't get hard. Her desperation tugged at me harder than Gunnir tugged at his dick.

Gunnir groaned. "Come on, girls. Get us hard."

"How?" Sam asked.

"Kiss," he said through a growl.

Ophelia and Sam looked at each other, but neither made a move. Gunnir tensed beside me and kept yanking his dick.

"Go on, Ophelia," I said. I didn't speak in a loving way, but she knew what she needed to do and that I was trying to help her, even if it didn't feel like it.

Ophelia played along like a good girl, leaning in and pressing her lips to Sam's. It was so forced and did nothing to help me, but it worked like a charm for Gunnir. Instead of getting hard from what was happening in front of me, my mind drifted to memories of Ophelia. The way she got frustrated when she realized she could have made a better move during checkers. How her breasts swayed and pulled together when she leaned over to snatch another one of my pieces away. That got me hard, and I stroked myself to the thought of her doing such an unsexual thing. Something that turned me on because it was Ophelia just being herself.

Gunnir's hand sped up and he lifted the saucer to catch his come. I focused on thoughts of Ophelia and leaned forward over the saucer when I came. With a satiated groan, Gunnir pushed his plate toward Sam, and the girls stopped kissing. I pushed mine in front of Ophelia.

Gunnir fastened his overalls and gripped the TV stand for balance as he hauled himself to his feet again. I stayed on my knees. He eyed the saucers for a moment and scratched at his double chin. "No, I don't think that's gonna do."

Ophelia's eyes went wide and leapt to me, but I couldn't look at her. Whatever Gunnir had in mind would crush her, and I didn't want to see that.

"Alex, when you think about an eating competition, the contestants have to eat more than that, right?" He turned his shit-eating grin toward me and walked to the fridge. "I mean, those girls can probably lap that up in two flicks of their tongues. There's not much sport in that."

Before his hand reached the busted handle, I knew what he had in mind.

The upper half of his body disappeared behind the refrigerator door, and he rummaged around for a moment. He knew exactly what he was looking for. He was only drawing it out to torture the girls more than he already had.

Realization dawned on Ophelia, and a small whimper slipped through her lips. That was all the encouragement Gunnir needed. He stood up with a mayo jar in one hand and a Coke bottle in the other.

"That's right," he said to Ophelia. "You remember this jar, don't you?" He wiggled it in the air and sent its gooey contents slopping against the glass.

She closed her eyes.

He pawed through a drawer and brought out two measuring cups. He turned to me. "You think a cup is enough?"

I glanced at the saucers. "I don't think those tiny plates will hold a whole cup, and I'm not cleaning our shit off the floor if it spills over."

"That's what *they're* for," Gunnir said, gesturing toward the girls. "They gotta eat it all, whether it goes on the floor or not."

"Just do half a cup, Gunnir. Damn."

Gunnir rolled his eyes and relented. As he squeezed the Coke bottle, the contents oozed out in thick globs. He tried to do the same with the mayo jar, but its sticky hold refused to let go. "Fucking A," Gunnir said. He put down the coke bottle, grabbed an old rubber spatula from a drawer, and scraped the sides of the jar, flinging the contents into the other cup. I paid attention to which one held my come. As I suspected, he went to tilt his cup over Ophelia's saucer.

"Wrong one, dumbass," I said.

Anger flared in his eyes, just as I'd hoped. If I could get him mad enough, he might abandon the game altogether and make a beeline for me. But it didn't work this time. He wanted to play this sick game more than he wanted to pummel my face. He swapped the cups and poured the aged come onto the correct saucers.

"Alright, ladies, hands behind your backs."

They stole a glance at each other before they interlocked their fingers behind their backs, took a deep breath, and leaned closer to the saucers.

"First one to clean their plate wins. Loser gets branded," Gunnir said.

Ophelia's eyes shot to me. I shook my head. I wasn't kidding her when I told her not to lose.

"Ready . . . set . . ." His twisted laugh cut through the tension, leaving them hanging over their plates like dogs waiting for the command to eat. "Go!" Gunnir hollered with a clap of his hands.

Ophelia hesitated, her hair drifting onto the plate, and I fought the urge to encourage her. I didn't want to see her perfect skin branded with a "B." *Come on, O,* I urged inside my head.

Ophelia licked at her plate, and my stomach tightened as hers lurched. She fought back gags as my cold come coated her chin. I drowned out Gunnir's sick encouragement and focused on Ophelia. Sam kept side-eyeing her to see who was ahead. Neither breathed through their noses, and air sputtered from their mouths between licks. Ophelia sat up a second before Sam, both their plates cleaned to a shine.

Sam whimpered as Gunnir grabbed her by the chain and unlocked her. He dragged her to the kitchen, heated the iron on the stove, and made the loser of his game face her punishment. Ophelia clutched her ears as Sam screamed, and I had to fight back the urge to cover my own, which was weird because I never shied away from their screams before.

The smell of burning flesh permeated the air and hung over us. In the mayhem, I grabbed Ophelia, unlocked her, and led her toward safety, but she couldn't stop looking back as she walked.

I brought her into the bedroom, closed the door, and pushed her against it. I brushed back her sticky hair and wiped the tears as they fell. "You did so good," I said. "Such a good girl." I pulled her into me until her body stopped lurching and the screaming in the other room quieted. I lifted her face, balancing her chin on my palm.

"I tried to let her win," she said between sobs. "She's been through so much. I thought I could take this punishment for her, but she wouldn't let me."

The hesitation. The way Sam kept watching her. I never realized just how brave Ophelia was until that moment. I pulled her against my chest and held her until her sobs quieted. "You really would have taken the brand?" I asked.

She shrugged and gave a weak laugh against me, but the tears surrounding it made it sound so hollow. "You already own me, and I already have scars. You can't see them, but they're there. What's one more?"

I held her away from me and looked into her eyes, afraid this game had broken her, afraid that her spirit had finally been crushed beneath Gunnir's cruelty. But what I saw before me wasn't a broken woman. The tears had dimmed the light in her eyes, but it still shined. How much more could she take, though?

She looked up at me, her lower lip quivering as the threat of more tears clouded her eyes. With shaking hands, she gripped the hem of her shirt and pulled it away from her body until she was down to only the boxers.

"What are you doing?" I asked. Was it some kind of test? If so, it wasn't fair. I'd fail.

"I want you, Alex," she whispered. "I go to other places in my mind when you take me because I need to escape what's happening around me. Now I need to escape what's happening by being taken." She took a step forward, pressing her bare chest against me, and waited for me to make my move.

She stood in front of me, wearing nothing more than my boxers, and I'd never seen something so beautiful. My gaze trailed up her body, and when I looked into her eyes, she looked more confident than when she knew she had the last move that would end our game of checkers. I would give her what she needed. What *I* needed.

I gripped her waist and pulled her with me as I sat on the bed, keeping her standing between my legs. I hooked my fingers into the waistband of the boxers and tugged them down her thighs. My lips moved to her lower stomach, and I circled my tongue around the sensitive skin. When I pulled her onto my lap, I brought my lips to hers, tasting the salty remnants of old come, and I could only think of her request as she straddled me.

She wants me.

Yeah, she made it seem like I was a distraction for her, but I didn't care because I'd never been wanted before. In any capacity. And she knew how much I wanted her. How much I'd always wanted her. Selfishly.

But I would be less selfish.

For her.

She lifted her hips, and I removed my boxers and lined myself up so she could lower herself onto me. I groaned as she slid down my length, engulfing me in her warm pussy and taking every inch of me inside her.

"Fuck, O," I growled.

Her head dropped into the crook of my neck, and the sticky ends of her hair brushed against my lips. I sucked her hair into my mouth, cleaning her of every reminder of what happened out there. When I released the strands, they were wet with my saliva instead of my come. I brushed her hair over her shoulder and lifted my hips to meet hers. The raw intimacy made my gut tighten with shame. This felt as wrong as it felt right. It went against everything in my very being. This closeness conflicted with everything I'd ever known before Ophelia. Women were to be used. They were soulless creatures who were hardly above a dog.

But that had been a lie. There was a soul inside Ophelia, and it beckoned me and encouraged me to find my own. Her body could be used while I still appreciated every curve of it.

Of her.

I raised myself to meet her and she came down on me. My hands fell to her hips as I let our bodies speak a language I'd never spoken. I'd never had a woman on my lap like that, chasing pleasure with her own speed and pressure. Having so little control over her felt foreign, but I welcomed the unknown.

My eyes kept moving to the door, expecting Gunnir to barge in and see what was happening. Ophelia on my lap, her velvet walls squeezing me as she grinded against me. Even with such a threat looming over our bodies, I didn't want to stop.

"Are you going to come, O?" I asked, but I knew. I felt the pulse of her excited heartbeat around my dick. The tensing and tightening that squeezed my base, coaxing my own orgasm forward.

"Yes," she panted.

"Come with me," I growled, raising my hips to give her something solid to grind against, to take us over the edge of a ledge we could never climb back to. "I want to feel you come around my dick for the first time. I need to feel it."

When her spasms stopped and the moans against my shoulder quieted, I kept her on my lap, staying buried inside her for as long as I could. But there was no time to bask in the moment. If Gunnir came in and saw what we were doing, he'd rain hell down upon us both.

"I'll figure out how to open the gates for you, O." I kissed the top of her head. "I promise."

CHAPTER EIGHTEEN

OPHELIA

Gunnir burst through the door and startled us awake. His lip curled back with disgust at the sight of us in bed together.

Alex sat up and rubbed his eyes. "What the hell, Gunnir?"

Gunnir tossed a dress at me and threw makeup on the floor in front of the bed.

"We're having a party tonight." The look of disgust faded from his face, replaced by a grotesque smirk.

Keeping the blanket clutched around my bare chest, I lifted the dress from the floor and laid it on the bed. I turned to Alex, silently begging him to stop this before it went any further. Alex tensed beside me but stayed put.

Gunnir could sense the dissension, and he spat words at me that contradicted his sweet tone. "Don't think you can get out of this. I don't care if you want to do this. *I* want to." He smiled. "Now do your makeup all pretty."

I knew in my gut this wasn't a party for me. It wouldn't be a party at all.

"Alex, get your pathetic ass out of bed and help me," Gunnir snarled before turning to leave. "Now!" he yelled from the hall when Alex didn't move.

Alex gave my shoulder a reassuring squeeze and left. After the door clicked shut behind him, I rose to my feet on legs made of Jell-O and lifted the dress again. It was a cheap black lace dress, and it was short as hell. I groaned and picked through the scattered makeup. I hadn't used any since the night at the diner, and I wouldn't have chosen any of these brands or colors. The cheap powder was too light, the mascara would probably give me an eye infection, and the lipstick was a gaudy shade of red.

I stripped off my flannel shirt and put on the dress, the hem of which stopped just past the juncture between my legs. I owned underwear that offered more coverage than that. I looked in the mirror and unscrewed the mascara top. I couldn't help but wonder how many people had used it before me. How many had died with it clumped around their eyes? I coated my lashes, and they curled upward, fanning around my blue eyes. My hair was a mess of tangles from washing it without brushing through the knots first. I tried to run my hand through it to get out the snarls, but it was no use. I was as much of a mess as I felt. I didn't bother with the powder or lipstick.

When Alex came back in, his breath caught in his throat at the sight of me. He changed into a nice shirt and slacks, his eyes never leaving me. He looked so handsome in something other than flannel, and I almost said so out loud. Then I remembered that I'd had to lick his come off a saucer like a goddamn dog.

I wasn't upset with him because of what had happened, though. He'd done all he could to protect me, and I hadn't been forced to lick up Gunnir's vile come. At least Alex's was familiar. It was tolerable.

"My fucking God, O," he whispered as he grazed my arm. "You're beautiful."

I didn't feel very beautiful, but the way he looked at me almost made me believe it. He leaned close to my lips, but he pulled away when heavy footsteps pounded down the hall.

The bedroom door rushed open, and Gunnir popped his head inside. "Don't tell her about the party favors," he said with a waggle of his finger.

My eyes rose to take in Gunnir's outfit. He'd changed into a suit as well, but it reminded me of a costume. Like a pig crammed into a cheap tux. From the smell emanating from his body, he hadn't bothered to shower, even for this festive occasion.

Alex led me to the living room, and my mouth gaped as I looked around. Balloons floated along the floor, banners hung across the doorways, and the island was set up with snacks and drinks in punch bowls. It reminded me of a cheap prom.

With tight lips, Alex gripped my shoulders and guided me onto the couch. Something was wrong.

Gunnir strolled over to the TV and flipped it on. A DVD screen came up before music began to play. Gunnir swayed his massive hips to the beat.

"Shouldn't you get your date?" Alex asked Gunnir.

"I should, shouldn't I?" He disappeared into the basement.

Alex leaned closer and spoke in a rush. "Don't drink anything I don't give you," he whispered before standing up and manning the island of food and drinks.

My eyes snapped to the door when I heard footsteps. Sam appeared, wearing a tight white dress that might have been shorter than mine. Fresh bruises covered her nose and cheeks, and the angry red brand blazed like neon on her thigh. A yellow crust had formed over it, and it must have hurt, because she favored that side with each pained step. I wanted to run to her, to reach out and hug her and let her know she wasn't alone in this, but I stayed planted on the couch. Gunnir sat Sam beside me. She kept her gaze straight ahead, but her hand floundered toward mine when her warden looked away. She gave my fingers a quick squeeze and pulled them back before he could notice.

Gunnir fiddled with the volume on the TV, raising it until the music thundered in my ears, drowning out my forming thoughts. He went to the wall, flipped off the lights, and turned on a disorienting strobe light. It flashed between colors and sent a wave of nausea through my body. Alex startled me when he came up behind me with a half-empty drink in a Solo cup. I shook my head, but he pushed it into my hand. When the light caught right, I saw that his glass was also well below the rim of the cup. He handed another cup to Sam, who took it with a learned trust—or an acquired carelessness. Who the hell knew after being stuck in this home for so long? Alex tilted the bottom of my cup, making me drink the tart liquor.

Gunnir plopped onto a chair with a Solo cup, sloshing dark liquid over his dress shirt. "Well, get up and dance," he said to us.

What the hell is happening?

Panic roared through me. I had no clue what was going on, but it didn't feel like something good. Nothing that Gunnir put together ever felt good, but this was somehow the worst yet. No amount of balloons or party decor could disguise the heaviness hanging above our heads like a guillotine.

When Sam and I stayed seated, Gunnir pointed at Alex's belt and Alex ripped it from the loops. His face transformed into something I hadn't seen in a while. Something feral and dangerous. I was almost certain he was putting on an act in front of Gunnir, but the intensity in his glare was so real.

We got to our feet, letting the music guide us as we

danced. I forced my hips to jerk in small movements, trying not to draw attention to myself. Sweat beaded on Sam's forehead as she lifted an arm and danced sensually to the beat. Her eyes were closed, as if she was far away in her mind. Every time I grazed her thigh, she winced, but she didn't respond to anything else. She just swayed with her head dropped back.

Alex sat on the couch, his eyes locked on mine. Sweat began to gather on my forehead. I couldn't understand it. I only drank half a cup of that home-concocted punch, and I wasn't drunk. This felt different from the heaviness alcohol brought. It was an odd lightness. Sweat collected and glistened on Sam's chest. When I looked at Gunnir, he gazed at us with a glassy-eyed stare. My eyes met Alex's, and he had a faint shine of sweat on his forehead. He smirked and shrugged out of his jacket.

Something was in the drinks, and it wasn't just alcohol.

Had he tricked me? Had last night been a lie to lull me into a false sense of trust?

"You girls get closer now," Gunnir said as he downed the rest of his drink.

Sam squealed and did the same, dropping her empty cup to the floor once she'd guzzled the rest of the liquid. My skin flamed with heat as Sam drew closer and rocked her warm, sweat-covered body against me. She smelled like the basement —like *captivity*—and the nauseating perfume made me want to vomit. My body thrummed as the music took on a life of its own in front of me, dancing along the walls like shadows made from firelight.

Gunnir groaned from his chair, and I felt the rumble of his throat from across the room. I felt everything.

"Kiss," Gunnir commanded.

I shook my head, but Sam clumsily turned toward me and looked up at me with haunting blue eyes. When I looked back at Alex, his smirk had turned sadistic. When I mouthed the word *no* to him, he tapped the belt on his lap. I felt alone in this hyper-charged room of emotions. I was suffocating. The shadows on the walls leapt from the aged paint and came to life. Their dark shapes skittered along the floor, moving away whenever I tried to look directly at them.

Sam's hot hands caressed my cheeks and broke me from my panic. Her lips were on mine before I could react, her fingertips hooking my hair as her kiss deepened. She tasted even more like captivity than she smelled, like she had just finished sucking Gunnir's dick before she came to this "party." Or maybe it was the sweat coating her skin. I blocked those thoughts and allowed myself to get lost in her kiss, melting into her touch as it moved along my body.

When I turned back to Alex, he looked off. His eyes were heavy, and he seemed as lost as I was. I saw movement from the corner of my eye. It was Gunnir, his eyes locked on us as he stroked his dick through the unzipped opening in his slacks. Heat pressed against my back, and I shook my gaze from Gunnir and pulled away from Sam's kiss. Alex stood behind me, his hand on my hip. He pressed a filled cup toward my hand and removed the empty one I forgot I'd been holding. Without hesitation, I turned up the cup and expected more of the odd liquid. Instead, I bathed in the refreshing coolness of water as it dribbled from the corners of my mouth.

Sam's hand rode up my inner thigh with a flirty touch. Alex got between us and whispered something in Sam's ear. Like a blind moth trying to seek out light, she stumbled to Gunnir and dropped to her knees in front of his feet. Her head lowered to his lap.

I turned back to Alex and whispered, "What's going on?"

Alex grabbed my waist and tugged me into him. His hips moved with mine as he leaned toward my ear. "We're fucking high," he whispered.

"What?"

"Psychedelics. I don't know about you, but I'm fucked."

It all made sense. The shadows. The sweat. But why?

Before I could ask the question, he answered it. "We're high, but they aren't even on the same planet," he said. "Come get more water. You need to sober up."

He grabbed my hand and guided me to the sink, away from the thumping music that wormed its way into my brain. He filled a cup and drank it before filling it again and handing it to me.

"What the hell is going on?" I asked after gulping the liquid. It felt as if I'd never drink enough water to satisfy my body's needs.

"Diversion. For us."

"What does that even mean?"

"The whore and Gunnir got twice the dose we did."

"Her name's Sam," I corrected.

Alex nodded and drew my hips toward his as he leaned back against the counter. "There were much bigger plans for you two tonight, but I couldn't let Gunnir go through with what he wanted to do."

"My knight," I quipped.

"You have no idea what I had to do to keep you from getting fucked by me, my brother, and probably the wh—I mean Sam, too."

I leaned over the island and looked toward the living room. Sam pawed at Gunnir's lap, her eyes half open, and Gunnir let his dick go as his eyes lolled. They were both gone.

"Can we leave?" I asked.

He shook his head. "Not yet. It's not that simple."

"It looks pretty fucking simple to me. He's out of his gourd. We could tap dance out the door and he wouldn't realize what was happening."

"Lower your voice," he whispered. "I know it's hard to understand, but he's still my brother. I need more time to figure this out." He shook his head. "For starters, I would need time to get this shit out of my system before I could drive us out of here, and we can't take off down the road on foot. That would draw too much attention. I'll set you free and I'll even go with you, but I'm not willing to bring the law to his doorstep. He can't hunt women if I'm not here to help him. He'd no longer be a threat."

I looked back at Sam. "And what about her? I can't just leave her, Alex. Not after everything she's done for me."

He shrugged his shoulders and drank more water. "Then we take her with us if you think she can keep her mouth shut."

"I know she can. I'll get her a job at the diner and—"

"What are y'all doing over there?" Gunnir shouted from the chair.

Alex pulled the cup from my hand and jiggled it in the air. "She needed more of that punch." He looked at me and whispered, "Play along."

Alex pulled me toward the living room and pushed my back against the wall. Its surface cooled my sweaty skin. His hands rode up my thighs and raised my skirt, then he worked open his slacks and pulled out his cock. When he pushed inside me, a deep growl left his lips, and I swear it crawled along the floor toward his brother, because it made Gunnir perk up. His small eyes were on me as Alex raised my leg and pushed deeper. When he knew his brother was watching, he fucked me with a possessive show of force that made me ache. When his brother looked away, he stayed inside me, basking in my heat with his face buried in the crook of my neck. He inhaled my scent and sighed.

With Gunnir hard once more, he dragged Sam onto his lap and positioned her over his stubby dick. Sam's eyes lolled toward the back of her head as Gunnir held her waist and used her body as if she were a doll. I closed my eyes and let myself feel lost in the moment. I focused on Alex inside me and pretended we were anywhere else. Somewhere where I didn't have a chain around my neck and I wasn't a captive in their home.

When I opened my eyes, what I saw made me hope I was witnessing a hallucination from a bad trip. Sam groped in her cleavage for something. She found it with a smile and gripped it between her pale fingers. The nail. The one I had tossed away after I stabbed Alex. My mouth dropped open as her fist flew toward Gunnir's eye socket. He stopped her with a firm grip on her wrist, leaving little more than a millimeter between the pointed end and his eye. He shook the nail from her hand and brought his hands to either side of her head. With his dick still inside her, he snapped her neck.

Sam's body fell forward. Even as she grew cold against him, Gunnir continued pumping his hips. He didn't push her off his lap until he was finished. A full-body shiver raked my spine as Gunnir's gaze went from Sam's body to us. He rose to his feet and started toward Alex's back.

I tried to get out Alex's name, but his brother moved with a speed I'd never seen. He ripped him away from me and threw him to the ground, leaping on top of him before Alex could register what was happening. "That's your whore's fault!" he screamed as he pointed to Sam's body. His angry gaze leapt to mine. "That nail came from you."

Alex's eyes widened for a moment, taking in the scene in front of him. Sam was dead, Gunnir's cock was still exposed, and the anger in the room suffocated me until I wondered if I would die next.

"What happened?" Alex asked.

Gunnir gritted his teeth and grabbed Alex by the shirt. "She tried to stab me with that nail your bitch used on you, so I broke her fucking neck!"

Alex's eyes narrowed. "Gunnir, she didn't do that. You did," he snarled as he tried to wriggle from beneath his brother's stern grasp. "Take responsibility for it. You got that girl to the point where she wanted to kill you because of *you*."

Gunnir drew his arm back and punched Alex in the face, but once wasn't enough to quiet his rage. His fists rained down on his head, beating him until blood ran from Alex's nose and stained his white dress shirt. Gunnir didn't stop until Alex's head lolled to the side and he went motionless beneath him.

I was stuck, frozen against the wall as the scene played out in front of me. I kept hoping it was a bad trip, but every time the strobe lights flashed over Sam's body, the harsh reality was too concrete to deny.

Gunnir turned toward me with a cruel smile, white droplets of spit flying from between his teeth with each panting breath. "We're alone, girl," he said as he climbed to his feet and stepped into me. I whimpered as he threw a fist through the wall by my head. "Look what you made me do." He pointed toward Sam's body. "You had something to do with that, didn't you? You may have been able to get into Alex's head, fuck him like you're his girlfriend or something, but that's gonna end tonight." He licked his lips before fisting my hair and craning my neck.

"Please don't," I begged, but a darker look filled his eyes. He wasn't human, and no amount of pleading would do a damn thing to save me.

Gunnir gestured toward Alex's body. "Bet you didn't know that he doesn't like to be called Alex, huh? He wants to forget he's a Bruggar that fucking bad. Forget that he had to be whipped into taking the family name seriously. Did he tell you that? Just how much we tried to beat the pussy out of him? All those marks on his back was from being set on fire. A little gas and a match was all it took for him to finally admit who he was. A fucking Bruggar. Fuck him like he's not a Bruggar all you want, girl, but know that's who he is. That you're willingly letting a monster into your cunt."

Gunnir growled and forced my head against the wall. My skull broke through the drywall and sent dust and chunks crumbling to my feet. The hit made me dizzy, and I blinked hard to stop my sight from doubling.

"Believe it or not, I care about him. I won't fuck you, but you're gonna help me get him over his little problem with come."

Gunnir pushed his weight against me and stroked his dick. His slimy tongue flicked out of his mouth, dangerously close to my lips, and I fought the urge to turn my head. It would have pissed him off even more. Sour breath rushed across my cheek as a low groan left his throat. He came in the palm of his hand, and tears overflowed from my clenched eyes as he rubbed his come between my legs, pushing his fingers inside me and slapping my pussy before tugging his hand away.

"Go on. Get him hard and get on his dick."

I shook my head.

"Get!" he yelled, and dug his wet fingers into my thigh.

I walked over to Alex and leaned down, and he murmured something that was too low to hear over the music. Gunnir came up behind me and whipped my lower back with Alex's belt. I screamed out, reaching back to baby the curve of my spine. Without any other option, I straddled his waist. He was limp at first, but he began to respond to my heat, even while hurting.

"Atta girl," Gunnir said as I leaned forward and put Alex inside me.

"I'm sorry," I whispered in Alex's ear, though I had no idea why I was apologizing. Maybe because I knew it would hurt him worse than the beating he'd received.

"Come on, girl. I know you can ride a dick better than that," Gunnir said as he raised the belt.

I moved on Alex's lap, and the wet sound between my legs intensified. Alex came to and tried to stop my movements by placing a rough hand on my thigh. He blinked heavily as he tried to get up with me on his lap.

"O," he whispered.

"How does it feel, Alex?" Gunnir asked, dropping to his knees and leaning closer to his brother.

"What?" Alex asked, wiping the blood from his nose.

"My come inside her." Gunnir stared at me and licked his lips.

"What the fuck, Gunnir!" Alex screamed as he threw his hip upward and knocked me to the ground. I hit my head on the hardwood floors and yelped. Alex jumped onto wobbling legs as he wiped at his dick. He grabbed Gunnir by the collar of his jacket. "What did you do to her?"

"I didn't fuck her, if that's what you're worried about."

"You sick fuck." Alex threw a punch to the oaf's face, and the big bastard fell to the ground, then he sent his boot into Gunnir's stomach, knocking him onto his back. Gunnir let out an eerie laugh and made a show of lapping the blood that drifted too close to his lips.

Alex reached toward me, and I took his hand. As I rose to my knees, my eyes locked on Sam. She looked so caught off guard, so serene. Like she was high as hell when she was killed. Hopefully she'd been somewhere else in her mind, which was a good thing, I guess. My stomach tightened. Her last moments had been spent with Gunnir inside her. My heart sank in my chest as her blue eyes stared hauntingly ahead. Alex pulled me away and aimed me toward the bedroom.

"This isn't over!" Alex yelled over his shoulder as he pushed me into the room and slammed the door.

I clutched my head, trying to ignore the headache building behind my eyes. Before I knew what was happening, Alex removed his shirt and pulled me into his broad chest. The hum of his heart thudded against my ear.

ALEXZANDER

A BLINDING red rage pulsed within every cell in my body. Gunnir had gotten the upper hand, but I never expected him to do what he'd done. Was I really surprised, though? No. Not in the slightest.

"What the hell happened?" I dared to ask.

"I don't know . . ." she said with a shake of her head.

"You do, so talk to me." I tried to calm my voice for her sake, but I was yelling in my mind.

She looked at the floor. "He came in his hand and rubbed it all over me. Inside me . . ."

"He didn't fuck you?" I raised her chin until her eyes met mine. "None of this is your fault. You can tell me."

She shook her head. "No, he didn't." Her chin quivered. "But he killed Sam."

I should have expected it. When Gunnir got mad, he lashed out at whatever was in arm's reach, just as our father had. But why he'd killed her, one of the few captives who'd somewhat tolerated him, was beyond me.

Tonight went so wrong. It didn't go according to anyone's plan. Gunnir intended for both girls to get fucked up from their drinks, leaving us sober enough to enjoy them with each other before branching off. My goal was to keep Ophelia safe, so I took half of her drink and poured it into Gunnir's. But as the evening shifted, Gunnir became more unhinged. I didn't expect him to kill anyone because of it, though, and I sure as fuck didn't expect him to push his come inside Ophelia just to prove a point. Fuck him.

I guided Ophelia to the bathroom and washed the blood off my face while she shifted her weight on both feet. "Can I shower?" she asked.

I nodded. I didn't want his come to dry on her perfect skin any more than she did. I wanted all traces of him off her. She stripped off her dress and I released her chain so she could get in the shower. She didn't even close the curtain. She just leaned under the stream and let the water wash over her.

"I'm sorry, O," I said, but I wasn't sure if she heard me. Gunnir violated her, and it was all because I couldn't protect her. I shouldn't have poked the bear.

Things were going to get so fucking ugly, and no amount of protection would keep Gunnir away from Ophelia, especially with no captive of his own to torment. The delicate balance was set to be disrupted.

And there was nothing I could do about it.

Chapter Nineteen

Alexzander

I threw the plate of supper in front of Gunnir without meeting his gaze. He hadn't tried to talk to me since he did what he did. I didn't even help him get rid of Sam's body. He wanted to kill her out of anger, so that was all on him. I also didn't care to see what he sometimes did to them once they were dead.

"A pussy is a pussy, even if they ain't breathing."

Yet another thing that differentiated us. Dead girls did nothing for me. No matter how much I used them when they were alive, I couldn't get hard once they grew cold and the blood hardened in their veins. The Man used a small space heater between their legs before he fucked them like that, but Gunnir didn't bother. He didn't need their warmth because their rapidly dropping temperatures matched his cold heart.

I sat down and tried to pick at my food. I thought about how Ophelia had felt on top of me in the bed. I wanted more of that.

The squelching sound of Gunnir's come broke through the memory and made my jaw tick. It was a low blow, even for Gunnir. He wanted to hurt me in the worst kind of way, and he had. I hadn't touched Ophelia since, leaving her locked in the bedroom like a dog that pissed where it shouldn't have. I felt bad about that because she hadn't done anything wrong. She'd been his victim as much as I had.

I pushed around the peas and gravy on my plate, too pissed off to eat.

"Alex, are you really still mad?" Gunnir asked.

I dropped my fork. "Call me Alexzander, Zander, or nothing at all," I snapped. Rage gripped my gut in a fist and squeezed.

Gunnir patted his belly after cleaning off his plate. "What's your problem?"

"You. You're my problem. You know I don't want you touching Ophelia, yet you not only rubbed your come all over her fucking pussy, you made me chase it. You know how I feel about that!" My anger grew, becoming white hot. I grabbed the knife from beside my plate and aimed it toward Gunnir. "Don't fucking touch her again."

Gunnir pushed my hand away. "So angry, little brother. The Man would be proud of you for gaining a pair of balls."

"Fuck you, Gunnir!" I sank the knife through Gunnir's hand with enough force to lodge it within the table's wooden innards. His head reared back, and he let out a scream. Blood spread around the blade, seeping into the wood beneath his pinned palm.

"You're dead!" Gunnir snarled. He gripped the knife handle and freed the blade from his flesh. I kept my eyes on him as he wrapped his hand with a kitchen towel before heading toward his room.

With trembling limbs, I got to my feet and threw the knife in the sink. I didn't know what Gunnir would do next, but he was pushing me past my limits. I put the plates in the sink and went to the bedroom. Ophelia's eyes ran up my body. She started to tremble, probably because she felt the anger radiating from my skin like heat shimmer rolling off pavement. I wouldn't hurt her, though. She was the last one I wanted to hurt at that moment. I wanted to hurt myself or Gunnir, but not her. Never again.

"Why do you have blood on you?" she asked, her eyes falling to my wrist.

"Because Gunnir needs to learn to keep away from you. You aren't his to touch, and I was making sure he remembers that the next time he thinks about it." I pulled a dirty shirt from a small pile on the floor and wiped away the blood.

That seemed to calm her down, and her shoulders relaxed. "Why haven't you ever corrected me when I called you Alex?"

"What do you mean?"

She played with the hem of the flannel shirt engulfing her small frame. "Gunnir said you don't like to be called Alex, and I heard you tell him to stop calling you that. What do you like to be called?"

I shook my head. "I don't care what you call me, but it pisses me off when Gunnir calls me Alex. That's what my mother called me. It's different when you say my name, though."

She stopped playing with the shirt and let her arms fall to her sides. The curves of her breasts pulled the top of the fabric taut, and my mouth watered. I stepped back and brushed a hand through my hair. I wanted her. God, I fucking wanted her, but I couldn't stop thinking about Gunnir claiming her *and* me with his come.

"Fuck, O." My voice came out in a husky whisper.

"What?" she asked. She rose to her feet and her eyes stared through my soul.

"I can't get past what he did to you last night."

I wanted to claim her again, but the nagging reminder that I was a Bruggar kept my feet sewn to the floor. I was The Man's son. It wouldn't be enough to sink into her again. I would need to take her. I leaned over my dresser and tried to stop myself from erasing all the progress I'd made.

She stayed silent behind me. When the turmoil in my mind settled to a whisper and my vision became my own again, I turned to face her.

"You can't get past it?" she asked. "What he did . . . what he made me do . . ."

In two strides, I met her where she stood and pulled her into me. "No. This has nothing to do with you, and you don't deserve to feel like you've done anything wrong. I'm not upset with you at all. It's more than you can understand."

She pulled back and looked up at me. "So tell me. Help me understand."

"No matter who you want me to be or who you think I am, I can never be what you deserve. Even if it's not my fault, even if this is a disease someone else injected into my veins, I'm still harboring a sick infection."

"The Man," she said. "He did this to you. You have to see that. It's not who you are."

"It's not who I want to be, but it's who I am. Why can't *you* see *that*? I kept hurting people, even after—" I stopped myself from going any further. She didn't need to know what I'd done, because she'd only see it as proof of my desire to be good instead of evil.

"Don't close up," she said. "Keep talking. It's not like I can run away once you spill your secrets." She lifted the chain and gave it a wiggle.

"It's not that easy, O. No one knows this, not even Gunnir." I sucked in a deep breath. I didn't want to talk, didn't want to admit the cowardly act that would make me a hero in her eyes, but she silently pleaded for me to give her this vulnerable part of me. And I couldn't deny her. "What I'm about to tell you . . . I didn't do it for courageous reasons. I need you to understand that. I did it out of fear. I did it because I was a selfish, angry, and terrified person."

She looked up at me and gripped my hands in hers. If I'd seen pity or admiration in that moment, I'd have stopped right there. Instead, I saw acceptance. Understanding. It was enough to spur me on.

"The Man had chained me to the floor and kept me there for almost a week because I refused to follow his come after he brought a new girl home. For seven days, he only offered me water and harsh words. On the seventh day, he brought her into the room and unchained me. He and Gunnir had both had their way with her, and he said my only way out of that room was to do what needed to be done."

Tears glossed Ophelia's eyes. She squeezed my hands, encouraging me to tell it all. ·

"He left the room, but I couldn't do it. It wasn't just following his come that stopped me. It was the pain on her face. The fear. How could I hurt someone when I knew what it meant to be hurt?"

She opened her mouth, and I stopped her before she said what I knew she'd say.

"Don't. It doesn't mean I'm a saint. I'm just as much a devil as The Man and Gunnir."

Her mouth closed. She'd give me that.

"When she realized I wasn't going to do anything to her, she looked out the window. 'Do you see those flowers?' she asked. I turned my head and spotted a tall patch of white. 'That's hemlock,' she said. 'If you get me a handful of it, I'll pretend you did what he wanted you to do so that you can get out of here.'"

"Did you know?" Ophelia asked.

"That hemlock was poisonous?"

She nodded.

"Yeah, I knew." I swallowed down the memory before allowing it to take shape again. "My mom had asked for it once, but when The Man saw me bringing her a clump of it, he knocked it out of my hands, explained why she wanted it, and beat the shit out of me for taking orders from a whore."

When I closed my mouth and didn't continue, she gave me a gentle nudge. "Keep going."

I pushed my mother from my mind and soldiered on. "She was as good as her word. She kept up her end of the bargain and when I got out of that room, I kept up mine. I didn't just pull enough hemlock for her, though. I took some for myself. I stuffed it in my pockets and planned to make a nice tea with it once I'd paid her for her help. Figured I'd sit in the living room and sip it while we watched the evening news."

Ophelia sucked in a breath.

"I snuck into the basement and handed off her share. Told her to wait until later in the night. The Man was well on his way to being drunk, and I didn't want him to find her until the next day. When I went to make the tea, The Man hollered for me to bring him some food. That's when it hit me. I could get rid of the problem."

"You put the hemlock in his food, didn't you?"

I nodded.

"Didn't he taste it?"

I shrugged and shook my head. "If he tasted it, he never said anything. He was probably too drunk."

As hard as it was, I told the rest of it. How he'd started to sweat and convulse. How Gunnir had rushed into the room and asked what had happened. How I'd said he was choking, and the idiot believed it. How Gunnir had hollered for me to perform the "Hemlock Maneuver" and how I'd fought to hold back a fit of laughter because the irony of his word choice nearly sent me over the edge. How I'd smiled as the man suffocated on his own vomit.

When I finished, Ophelia pulled me into her and rested her head against my chest. "I don't think you were brave for doing that," she said. "If you had been brave, you would have finished off your brother and ended the whole mess. You never would have taken another woman. You never would have taken *me*."

She understood without having to be told. I'd killed him to save myself, not anyone else, and I hadn't even done *that* right. I'd stayed with Gunnir and kept doing the things I hated because it was all I knew. And even knowing all this, she pressed herself against me because she believed I could be better. Even though a disease saturated my soul, she believed I could be healed.

I tilted her chin, looked into her eyes, and vowed to myself that I'd go no further than a kiss. I wouldn't be like The Man. I would be the man she saw in me.

I leaned into her and captured her mouth with my own. My hands rested against the soft, warm pulse in her neck, and I stepped into her until her back pressed against the wall. I kissed her. Our mouths moved together, soft and slow, but with an undercurrent of hunger that wasn't a one-sided need. I tasted it on her tongue, heard it in the soft whimper against my lips. I could claim her in a way The Man and Gunnir could never claim a woman. She was mine because she *chose* to belong to me.

A crash beyond the bedroom door pulled me away from her perfect mouth. "Stay here," I said.

I left the bedroom and entered the hall. Another crash sounded from the living room, and I aimed my feet toward the noise. When I rounded the corner, I saw Gunnir with a bat in his hands, standing over the shattered corpse of what had once been a lamp. He turned with a primal grunt and swung the bat over the coffee table, snapping it in two.

"What the hell are you doing?" I asked.

When he turned toward me, his eyes were bloodshot and glossy. "I got nothing left, so no one should have nothing!" He brought the bat down on the splintered table again.

I closed my eyes and took a breath. I knew he would feel that way once he realized what he'd done. Once he realized he was alone without his captive and that he'd pushed me too far.

"You did all that, Gunnir. No one else."

Gunnir's gaze met mine, and a fiery anger settled across his face. "It's your fault."

"How?"

"Because we ain't supposed to like the girls. We ain't supposed to get attached. They're objects, with no more worth than this fucking lamp or table." Gunnir pointed the bat at the shattered remains on the floor.

I shook my head. "I'm not attached."

I was lying, and he knew I was lying. I let myself get attached to Ophelia after a lifetime of avoidance. Ophelia shined. Like a little ball of light in a world of darkness, she illuminated the hidden places and chased the shadows away. I was realizing—much too slowly—that I'd do anything for her, including becoming someone other than the demon brought into the world by the devil himself.

Gunnir screamed, took a wide stance, and swung the bat with all his strength. It collided with the old television and sent a spray of glass across the floor. "You're a fucking liar! I see how you two look at each other. She moves with you instead of against you when you fuck her."

He was right. Ophelia had escaped to some other place in

her mind when she first came here, but that had changed. She no longer needed to travel outside of herself. She didn't lift her hips away from me, trying to put distance between her skin and my touch. When I had her against the wall the night before, she'd pushed toward me, inviting me deeper. She wasn't disgusted by me even though I was disgusting. Everything about this place was disgusting.

I shrugged my shoulders. "I don't know what to tell you, Gunnir. I'm not any less of a Bruggar because I don't need them to hate me when I fuck them. It feels better when they don't."

"Pussy," Gunnir snarled. "The Man would be rolling in his grave if he heard you talk like that."

"That may be true, but our mother would be proud, and the devil's disappointment doesn't mean nearly as much as an angel's pride."

Gunnir gestured toward me with the bat and stormed down the hall toward his room. I didn't follow him. What I'd said had cut him deep, and if I went after him, he was liable to bring that bat down on my skull. I was about to retreat to my room and check on Ophelia when I heard rattling coming from his room. He could have been searching for another weapon, so I froze at the corner and waited. If he went for Ophelia, I could jump on his back before he got to her. If he went for me . . .

A closet door slammed and Gunnir popped out of his room with his arm behind his back. I backed up as he walked toward me with a crazed look in his eyes. My gaze wanted to leap to my bedroom door, but that would give him an idea. If I wanted to protect Ophelia, I had to keep him coming at me.

And he did. The corners of his mouth lifted into a smile, the arm behind his back fidgeting and wiggling around, situating something in his hand. It wasn't his hunting rifle—

I'd have seen the stock or the barrel poking out, even around his massive body—but it could have been The Man's pistol. Still, I stood my ground until he came within six feet of me and whipped his hand from behind his back.

It was a skull. Empty sockets stared at me, and yellowed teeth grimaced in an eternal smile. The flesh had long since disappeared.

Gunnir tossed it up and caught it. "Do you know what I like to do sometimes, Alex?" he asked.

I shook my head. Did I really want to know?

He gripped the bat with his other hand, and for a moment I thought he'd toss the skull in the air and hit it like a macabre baseball. Instead, he placed the bat on the ground between his legs, unclipped his overalls, and let the wad of denim fall to his knees. As his thumb stroked the skull, his other hand stroked his hardening dick. With his eyes on mine, he brought the skull to his crotch and pushed into the right eye socket with a deep groan. My lip curled, but he kept going, swapping his thrusts to move the skull up and down his meager length.

"Do you know who this was?" he asked through a groan I knew too well.

I shook my head. It could have been anyone. We'd dropped countless women into the pit over the years, and I couldn't think of one he favored enough to keep like this.

A deep grunt rose from his gut, and his hips stuttered as he coated the skull with his come. "It's our mother."

I was almost too stunned to react. "What?" I asked, my fists clenching at my sides. Had I heard him right? I couldn't have. That was an act far more disgusting than anything he'd done before.

Gunnir placed the skull on the mantle. The come dripped into the empty space where a nose would have been. "I skull fuck our mother, Alex," he said with a smirk. "She made you a little pussy, and this is my way of repaying her. You should want to disrespect her remains, too. Look what she did to you. Does your whore remind you of our mother? Is that what you like about her?"

I saw red. Every shade in bright clarity. I had protected him all this time because he was my brother. The last living tie I had to my mother. But he had never been a part of her. She had birthed him from her body, but he was merely a parasite placed inside her by The Man. I was done protecting him.

Gunnir patted the mantle. "The thing about these women, Alex, is that they all become a bag of fucking bones in the end. And your whore is no different."

Anger tore through me. I charged forward and dove for the bat. I managed to get my hands on the grip but as I struggled to my feet, his hands encased my forearms and prevented me from readying it for a swing.

"Fuck you!" I yelled as we tumbled into the wall. Drywall crumbled around our feet.

He backed away a step, but the wall prevented me from raising the bat over my shoulder. Before I could move away, he rammed his weight into my gut, sending me to the floor in a breathless heap.

His greedy fingers snatched away the bat. "I'm going to have fun fucking her before I kill her, Alex."

Gunnir raised the bat and brought it down on my head. Pain shot through my skull, and a soundless scream clawed its way up my throat. My heartbeat thumped rhythmically in my ears . . . or was that the sound of Gunnir's receding footsteps?

Ophelia.

I had to protect her.

I hauled myself to my knees and the floor pitched beneath me, sending me into the wall. I touched the back of my head, and my fingers met with a warm, sticky spot. For a moment I forgot I had arms and legs as I rolled onto my back and looked up at the ceiling. My head lolled to the side, and I spotted the bat, a red streak smeared across the tip. The sharp ringing in my ears receded, and muffled screams drifted from the hall and doubled in my brain. Desperation ripped through me as I forced myself to my knees again and crawled toward those familiar noises—muffled whimpers and the rhythmic sounds of a scuffle. It was coming from the far end of the hallway.

Gunnir's room.

I got to my feet, blinking to clear the blurry fog that painted everything. A wave of disorientation swirled around my legs, and I stumbled against the wall. Steadying myself, I continued toward my room. Sunlight burst through the window and blinded me, and I covered my eyes with a shaking hand. It didn't help. I clenched my eyes shut and felt my way across the room until I found the closet. I reached around, trying to grasp cold metal, but my fingers only met with cardboard, cloth, and dust. When my hand finally wrapped around the shotgun, I breathed a sigh of relief and started toward the dresser. Still unwilling to open my eyes, I groped through the drawer until I found the shells. My fingers hardly worked as I struggled to load the tube.

Normally I would have racked the gun once I got behind him. The noise would have been enough to scare him and stop whatever he was doing. Make him think twice. If what I thought was happening was in fact happening, however, I had no intention of just scaring him.

I racked the gun.

Keeping the weapon at my side, I stumbled down the hall. Wood cracked as I kicked open the door and entered a room that felt like my childhood, like the day I found my dead mother. My jaw ticked.

Ophelia was on her back on Gunnir's stained mattress, and she'd been stripped of all her clothes. His hand covered her mouth, and her nostrils flared in a frantic rhythm over his fingers. I focused on the worst things. His hand on her breast, the fabric of my flannel shirt ripped from her skin, his dirty overalls puddled around his boots. She turned her bloodshot gaze to me. She looked so scared, so fucking desperate. She couldn't even disappear within her mind because he was just that vile. The fear on her face showed me how trapped she was in that horrible moment, and my heart shattered in my chest, breaking into shards like the lamp Gunnir had destroyed.

He destroyed everything.

I raised the shotgun, trying to focus my blurred vision into a clear image. I knew what I had to do, and it wasn't just for Ophelia.

It was for me.

It was for my mother.

It was for all of us.

"Gunnir!" I screamed. He lifted his head away from her, a thick groan leaving his lips. Before he could turn around, before I could see his face and change my mind, I pulled the trigger.

The top of his head exploded in a shower of red. His legs crumpled beneath him, sending him onto the floor with a thud. Ophelia's screams tore through me. She scrambled backward on the bed and when her back hit the headboard, she just kept screaming. Blood and brain matter painted her skin.

I balanced against Gunnir's wooden dresser, trying to gather my bearings. The squelch of a bleeding head shot, Ophelia's screaming, and the echo of the gunshot created a nauseating mix of sounds that continued to play through my mind long after they'd stopped. I forced myself to pull it together for Ophelia. The shotgun slipped from my hand and clattered against the floor, and I went to her side. She was crying, her cheeks blazing red from his grasp on her mouth. She looked so fucking broken. I wrapped my arms around her and held her against my chest.

Now I had to do something that would be more difficult than ending my brother's life. I had to set Ophelia free and ensure no one would ever hurt her again. I had to destroy the last monster.

Me.

CHAPTER TWENTY

OPHELIA

I was in a vortex of emotions, each feeling swirling and connecting with the next until I couldn't pull them apart. My ears continued ringing from the gunshot. Gunnir's rough grasp was imprinted on my flesh, as if he still had his hand on my inner thighs as he spread my legs. I was glad the devil was dead, but also terrified about how it would affect Alex. He took his brother's life for me, but I wasn't sure if he'd done it to save me or to keep me all to himself. That weird familial competitiveness seemed generations deep.

I pushed away from his chest and looked into his eyes. Would he keep his promise? Would he open the gates for me? I would have my answer soon enough.

"Let's get you cleaned up," he said. He pulled away from me and turned to leave the room. A dark clump of blood matted his hair to the back of his head.

"Alex, you're bleeding," I said. "What did he do to you?"

He stopped in the doorway and gripped the frame with his

hand. He didn't turn to face me as he spoke. "It doesn't matter now. Come on. I'll run you a bath."

My inner thighs quivered when I rose to my feet. I'd strained the muscles by fighting to bring my legs together as Gunnir fought to tear them apart. When he'd entered Alex's bedroom with that crazed look in his small eyes, I'd known what I was in for. He'd tried to drag me to his room by my chain, but I gripped the leg of the bed and refused to let go. Then he'd lifted me over his shoulder, carried me to his room, and—

And I couldn't think about the rest. He hadn't gotten to me, but it had been too close.

As I headed toward the hall, I stopped at the foot of the bed and allowed my eyes to land on Gunnir's legs. I didn't want to look, but I *had* to. I had to know he wouldn't hurt me —or anyone else—ever again. My gaze stopped on the back pocket of his overalls. Something light peeked from the lip. Something blonde.

I stepped over a line of blood that had followed the track in the hardwood floor, and I knelt beside his feet, my hand trembling as it neared the keepsake tucked inside his pocket. As I pulled it out and realized what it was, tears sprang to my eyes. It was hair, about three inches and roughly cut, bound in the center with a rubber band. Sam's hair. A trophy for her killer.

I clutched it to my chest and apologized to the girl we hadn't saved.

"You coming?" Alex called from the bathroom.

I stood, walked to the bathroom, and placed the hair in Alex's hand. "Can you bury this with Sam's body? I don't want it to stay with your brother. He doesn't deserve to take any more of her than he already has."

Alex shifted on his feet. "He . . . didn't bury her, O."

I nodded. Of course he didn't. A burial would have been too civilized for someone like him. "Can you bury that, then?"

He tucked it into his pocket and left the bathroom. For the first time since I arrived in hell, I was granted privacy. It was a promising start, but I refused to get my hopes up. I still had a chain around my neck, after all.

I dug through the cabinet to the left of the sink, found a rag, and used it to wipe the crimson splatter from my skin before I climbed into the tub. The lukewarm soak would be bad enough without Gunnir's blood dirtying things. I stepped over the edge of the tub and submerged myself, skimming my fingers over the water's surface. When I'd had enough of wiping the memories from my skin, I rested my head on my knees and thought about all the times I'd been in this bathroom after some horrific incident. In some of those nightmares, Alex had been a key player.

When had that changed?

More importantly, when had *I* changed?

The shift had been as gradual as the sun's trek across the sky—imperceptible in the moment but undeniable all the same. I'd gone from wanting to end his life to seeing no life that didn't have him in it.

Alex returned with a towel and a change of clothes. "Hey," he said as he sat on the toilet beside the tub. He reached out and stroked my back with a gentle touch that sent a shiver through my limbs. "I'm sorry." His hand went to the back of his head, and he winced.

"Are you okay?" I asked.

"Don't worry about me," he said, drawing his hand from his head and sitting taller. "I'd have taken more of a beating if I thought it could have saved you from him."

"Why'd you do it?" I asked, flashing my eyes up at him.

"What do you mean?"

I couldn't look at him while pressing him further, so I focused on the water instead. "Why'd you kill him?"

Alex scoffed. "Because he touched you. I needed to save you from him."

If that were true, if he really wanted to keep me safe, he could have let me go. Instead, he'd tried to save everyone. But when he was forced to make a choice, he'd chosen me.

Why?

I drew my knees closer to me. "What am I to you, Alex?"

He shook his head. "I have no idea."

"How do you not know?"

"I have no way to know. How can I say I want to be with you or I love you when I don't fucking know what that means? Love has always hurt here, and I don't want to love you if it means I'll hurt you more than I already have." He sat without speaking for a moment, then he pulled something from his pocket and leaned toward me. His hands went to the chain, and the tinny click of the opening lock sounded like a cannon blast to my ears. As he pulled away, the weight of more than the hefty chain left my body. My eyes rose to his, and he wiped a single tear that had slipped down his cheek. "You're free now, O. The front door is open, just like I promised." Before I could respond, he placed the fresh clothes on the toilet, left the bathroom, and closed the door behind him.

I cleaned up, got out of the tub, dried my hair with the towel, and wrapped it around my body. I carried the clothes under my arm. When I stepped into the hall, my eyes darted toward the living room. Escape waited for me on the other side of the front door, but what would I escape to? I could only return to the hell I'd known before the hell I'd been transplanted into. Staying with Alex didn't seem much more promising. If he couldn't love me, if he didn't already feel something for me, there was no point. He hadn't even tried to get inside me since Gunnir pushed his vile come between my legs. What if Sam had been right? What if I was only useful to Alex as long as I was shiny and new?

I was at a crossroads, and both paths looked bleak.

Two roads diverged in a yellow wood . . .

My mind grasped at the long-forgotten Robert Frost poem I'd dissected for a project in high school. When faced with two paths, the man chose the road less traveled. He'd taken a chance and come out better because of it. Maybe the old poet was onto something.

Alex didn't know what love was, but I did. I could show him. He could come with me, and we could build a new life. Together. The money I'd stashed at my father's house wouldn't be enough to move to the city like I'd hoped, but it would be enough to survive for a month in the country while we figured out what to do next.

I walked across the hall and stepped into his room. He was lying on the bed, staring up at the ceiling. A look of surprise flashed across his face when he saw me. "I guess you didn't hear me. The door is open," he said before turning away from me. "Go, Ophelia." When I didn't leave, he turned over and narrowed his eyes at me. "Goddamnit, Ophelia, what do I have to do to get you to leave? This isn't a place for you."

"It's not a place for you either," I said, refusing to back down.

His eyes darkened. "This is exactly the place for me." He jumped to his feet, gripped my shoulders, and threw me onto the bed. My towel fell away and revealed my naked body, but I didn't try to cover myself. He climbed over me and spread my legs with his knees, but I didn't try to fight him off. With outstretched arms, he planted his fists on either side of my head. "This is who I am. This is who I will always be. Weren't you listening when I told you what happened after I killed The Man? I kept doing this because I can't stop!"

"You're just trying to push me away," I said, raising my chin.

"Because you *need* to be pushed away. You *need* to be afraid of me."

I shook my head. "It's my choice now. Not yours, and not anyone else's. What you're doing won't push me away. You can't fool me, Alex." My lip quivered, my strength and courage draining from me with the confession rushing past my lips. "You won't force yourself on me because that's not what you want. Even if it is, you won't do it because you haven't wanted me since Gunnir ruined me."

Hurt registered on his face like a slap. "Is that what you think? You think I haven't wanted to push inside you because of what Gunnir did?" He lowered his hips, pressing his hard length against me. "I've never stopped desiring you. I've never stopped *needing* you." He shook his head, his eyes softening when they met mine again. "You aren't ruined in my eyes. You're beautiful and broken, but you have the strength to pull yourself together. But if I go with you, I'll only break you again."

I closed my eyes and allowed the tears to fall. His words revealed more than he realized. He'd said I wasn't ruined, and while that admission brought me so much joy, what he hadn't said gave me something I needed even more: hope.

If he didn't see as ruined, there was only one reason he'd fought against his urge to devour me. Even though he couldn't admit it, the years of abuse hadn't left him damned beyond salvation. I saw him for who he was and who he could be. Now he just needed time to see it within himself.

"Come with me, Alex," I whispered. "Please."

He sighed and shook his head. "Where would we go?"

"Away. We can start over somewhere different. Somewhere that isn't here. I have a little money saved—"

He laughed and dropped his weight into me. "Do you

really think I can just walk out of here and forget about the place that made me this monster that I hate?"

He was right. Walking away wasn't enough. "Then don't just leave it. Burn it down. Burn it all."

He swallowed hard.

"You are not this place, Alex. No one owns you anymore. Not The Man or your brother. No one."

ALEXZANDER

OPHELIA WAS right on some things, but she was dead wrong on others. I belonged in that house. I deserved to be alone, with only my sins to keep me company. What other option did I have? Burn this place down and follow her to her father's house? This wasn't some fucked-up fairy tale where I would become a man instead of a monster once the spell was broken.

I had talked to her until I was hoarse, and she'd listened but hadn't heard me. She refused to save herself. If I wanted to keep her safe, I had to remove the threat. I had to do what I should have done all those years ago.

"Fine, get dressed," I said.

I climbed off her and stepped away from what I'd miss the most. Her mouth. Her kiss. The way she said my name. So much more. Everything. I left her in the bedroom so I could take care of business.

I dragged Gunnir from the house and dumped him into the bone pit. Only two canisters of gas remained in the barn because Gunnir had used one on Sam's remains. I needed one for him, which meant I'd only have one left for the house. It would have to be enough. I poured the gas into the pit and tossed down a match.

I emerged from the barn and saw Ophelia leaning against the truck, wearing a pair of my sweatpants and a sleeveless undershirt. It was weird to see her standing in a patch of sunshine. She looked so beautiful. And tired. And thin. I'd done that to her.

All the more reason for what I was about to do.

"Wait for me out here," I said. "I'll only be a minute."

It was selfish of me, but I leaned in and kissed her one more time. I didn't deserve to feel her soft lips or taste her again, but I'd never needed something so much in my life. As I pulled away, she looked up at me.

"Burn it down," she said.

I nodded. I would burn it down. I would destroy everything in that house that had hurt her.

I went back inside and splashed the noxious liquid throughout the house. I started in Gunnir's room, moved to my room, wound my way into the living room, and sat on the couch with an empty can. I had wanted to douse myself in gasoline, but I'd barely had enough to make it into the living room. This house had been the figurative hell for so many, and I was about to turn it into a literal inferno.

With a deep breath, I went to Gunnir's room and struck a match. It hit the bed with a rush of heat and flames that grew and consumed the mattress and dry wooden headboard. The dusty curtains behind the bed erupted in a flash of heat and light. I tossed the second match into my bedroom as I backed down the hall. A bright burst of fire reached into the hallway and settled into a warm glow. I continued my final tour, tossing matches into the kitchen before returning to the living room. I sat on the couch and threw more matches from my seat. I pulled a cigarette out of my pocket and lit one, letting it rest between my lips as the smoke mixed with the thick haze filling the house.

The overbearing heat pressed closer as I sat back and

puffed on the cigarette. My eyes grew heavy, and I dropped my head back and felt relaxed for the first time in a very long time. It was finally over.

"Alexzander?" said a voice in front of me. My mother's voice. *"Don't do this. You said you didn't know what love was, but you lied. The Man taught Gunnir hate, but I taught you love."*

"Fuck off, mother. You don't know all the horrible things I've done," I hissed back.

"It doesn't define you. What defines you is what you do now.
"

Heat seared my eyes, and I couldn't tell if it was from the flames or the tears threatening to fall. "What I'm doing now is taking myself out of the equation. I'll never hurt Ophelia again. I refuse to be like Gunnir and The Man for another day of my life."

"You aren't them. You have never been them, even when you've done things like them. They were without a conscience."

"I'm too damaged to be with her. I don't even know what drew me to her like this."

"She reminded you of me."

"That's not creepy or anything," I said through a cough. The cloud of smoke crawled along the ceiling, thickening with each passing second. I tried to sit up, but my head only lolled on a rubbery neck as sweat dripped into my eyes. I was too tired to wipe the sting away. "I'm trying to protect her."

"What about her father? Have you thought about how he'll continue to hurt her? You've cast that girl from the frying pan into the fire. Ophelia is good for you because she's shown you how different you truly are. She's brave, but she needs your strength like you need her softness."

I didn't speak. I couldn't. The fire had come close enough to heat my skin, and I was ready to receive my final punishment.

"Please, Alex. Don't go out like this. You deserve more than you think. She's lost like you. She needs you."

Hands gripped at me, and I tried to push them away with leaden arms.

"Alexzander!" The voice drifted from across a chasm, so far away. And it wasn't my mother's voice.

Ophelia.

Her hands tightened around my forearm as she tried to haul me off the couch, but I was an immovable weight. A hacking cough racked her chest. If I didn't do something, she'd succumb to the smoke while trying to save me. I lifted myself, forcing my legs to work beneath me because I couldn't allow her to die now after all she'd been through. I leaned my weight against her, supporting myself as much as I could, and we made our way to the door. The smoke thinned as we reached the threshold, and the air cleared the further we stepped away from the house.

She let me go and I collapsed onto the green grass, panting as I tried to inhale the fresh air. Ophelia looked like a fucking angel kneeling beside me, her hand rubbing against my sternum to encourage me to breathe.

"What the hell did you do?" she yelled.

"You wouldn't understand." The words rushed out in a wheeze. I turned onto my side and coughed until my chest threatened to split open. "You never should have gone in there after me. Do you know how stupid that was?"

"Says the man who decided to take a nap in a burning building." She sat back and coughed into the crook of her arm, then she dug into her pocket and placed the contents in front of me.

I looked at the items in disbelief. The picture of my mother. The drawing. The hair clip. I plucked them from the grass and clutched them against my chest.

"The game of checkers is already in the car. I grabbed this

stuff while you were in the barn." She smiled at me. "You're welcome."

"Thank you," I said as I pulled her into me and kissed her. "For everything." Another bout of coughs rattled through my chest.

"You need to go to the hospital, Alex."

I shook my head. "I've been through much worse than this."

I had nearly died more times than I cared to admit. At that point, I was worried I was actually immortal. Incapable of death. Destined to live with pain and torment for all eternity. And I still hadn't been able to prove otherwise.

Because of Ophelia. Because she'd refused to let me give up on myself.

And maybe that was a good thing. My mother's voice had brought up something I hadn't considered. There was another monster besides me in Ophelia's life, and I needed to take care of that if I wanted to keep her safe.

Chapter Twenty-One

Ophelia

Leaning against Alex's old pickup truck and staring at the burning house in front of us was almost empowering. The flames tried to destroy hell itself by lapping at the very bones of the structure that housed so much torment. Even though it seemed impossible, it was working. Engulfing, devouring, and cleansing the land of all the evil that was born and raised inside. Well, maybe not all of it. The man beside me had been spared.

Because of me.

Even though Alex was a part of them, I couldn't imagine him burning in that graveyard when he still had some signs of life. Some signs of humanity.

I lifted the hem of my shirt and wiped the sweat from my forehead. Alex reached over and wiped the trail of perspiration that rolled from my chest and slid down my belly. Goosebumps tightened my skin.

"I'd be dead if it weren't for you," he said, wrapping his hand around my waist and tugging me into him. He leaned in and kissed me. His breath smelled like smoke, like something ominous and dangerous. Like something that crawled from ash.

"And I'd be dead if it weren't for you," I whispered as I let his lips spread against mine.

"No, O. None of this would have happened if I hadn't abducted you."

I pulled away from him. He had no idea. "That's not true, Alex. Death was always on the table. Before you. With you. Maybe even after you. You forget what I've come from and what I have to go back to."

"No one else will ever touch you again." He reached out, wiping the sweat from my lower back and dragging my sweatpants down my thighs.

I stepped out of them and kept my hands clenched in fists at my sides, unsure about what was happening. I had wanted him to take me again, to prove that Gunnir hadn't dirtied me, but now that it was happening, I was so confused. There was no chain around my neck, no reason to comply to his demands, yet I wanted him as badly as he wanted me.

He lifted me until my legs wrapped around his waist. I balanced on the rusty fender as he backed me against the truck. He held me around his waist, unzipped his soot-covered jeans, and pulled out his cock. He pushed inside me with no inhibition.

Fucking outside of that home felt different. Almost wrong. Like I was allowing the chains to wrap around my heart.

Though we weren't right beside the house, the truck's metal had absorbed the fire's heat, and it burned the backs of my thighs as he fucked me. I watched the flames reach toward the sky, hissing as they consumed the shitty old farmhouse and all its shitty secrets.

The secrets pushing inside me now.

"Alex, stop," I said, the memories screaming as a fire of indecision scorched my soul.

He stopped, lifted my chin until my eyes met his, and shook his head. "No, O. You're mine, you will always be mine, and I need to claim your perfect pussy. I need to claim you outside of that house because *you* are my home now." He thrust inside me with enough force to take my breath away, then he gripped the truck's hood so he could fuck me harder. The way he needed to fuck me.

I watched the flames again, and another fire started inside me. Deep in my gut. I wrapped my arms around his neck and melted into him. I let him take my body. I let him own me like he wanted, and I began to accept and almost enjoy that ownership.

The friction rubbed between my legs, and the fire lapped at my insides, cleansing me of the hell that had resided within me for as long as I could remember. All the pain, hurt, and abuse that had tortured me long before Alex and his brother had taken me. It was like a controlled burn inside me, destroying the damaged earth of my soul and leaving the healthy growth behind.

I came around him, pulling his mouth to mine and filling it with my pleasure. His nails dug into the back of my thigh as my spasms drew his own.

"Come with me," I moaned against his mouth.

He did, and it was so fucking freeing. Sweat coated his chest and soaked my sleeveless shirt as he pressed against me, and I didn't care. We bathed in the heat and smoldered against the truck.

When he was sure I could stand on my own again, he retrieved the sweatpants. I steadied myself with my hands on his shoulders and stepped into them without bothering to clean up the mess between my legs.

He gave the house another glance and turned to me. "You ready to get out of here?"

"Definitely," I said with a nod. "Are you?"

His shoulders lifted in a noncommittal shrug. "I don't really have a choice. I just burned my house down," he said with a sly smirk.

A thought crossed my mind. "What about your neighbors? What if they call the police? Will anyone go looking for you?"

Alex shook his head. "No, we're miles from anyone else. This place used to be a pig farm, and it's got some acreage attached to it. The surrounding land is owned by farmers with a lot more acreage than us, so it shouldn't draw any attention. Folks around here keep to themselves. Some of them bring milk and eggs on occasion, but I can swing by and make something up before they show up again. Tell them we're planning to let the forest take the land back so we'll have more hunting area or something."

Why do you care? I asked myself. If this stunt landed him in jail, that would be one less moral dilemma to concern myself with. Yet I still cared and didn't know how to stop.

He tossed the keys at me, and I caught them and climbed in the cab. As we pulled away from the blaze, one thought kept running through my mind: Freedom felt weird. It felt even weirder to be beside Alex without a chain around my neck or the threat of Gunnir breathing down my neck. As he stared out the passenger-side window, I wondered if my version of freedom felt like captivity for him. He was willing to die in that house, so what could life possibly be like for someone like him?

We bumped along the potholes in the street, and I pushed the what-ifs from my mind. He directed me to the diner since I didn't know the backroads. Once the miles faded behind us and the diner came into view, I was back in familiar territory.

My home was a walkable distance from the diner, down a winding sideroad that disappeared into the thick wall of trees. I walked most nights because I lived for the peace and quiet of that walk, but I wasn't sure I'd ever go out on my own again, especially not on foot at night. I'd be too scared of being taken and brought back into the flames of hell. I'd be afraid of another monster like Gunnir.

A shiver raked my spine at the thought of him. I still struggled with the memory of what happened. When my father did things, I disappeared into my mind, usually to a park, sitting beneath the bright, warm sun. I could feel the heat of that sun instead of his hands. I heard birds chirping instead of his grunts and groans. I felt the grass prickling against the backs of my thighs instead of his weight pressing me into the mattress. I tried so hard to live in that park when Gunnir was over me, but he kept me trapped in the moment, forcing me to feel every unwanted touch. Then Alex entered the room, bleeding and armed, and he did what I couldn't. He saved me.

As we passed the diner, I began to process where we were heading. From one hellish home into another. The familiarity didn't make it any easier. I kept wondering if we'd walk in and find my daddy dead, eternally passed out on that beat-up recliner. I prayed the alcohol had killed him, but with my luck, he'd still be alive, waiting to prey on me like he always had.

My lip trembled.

"You okay?" Alex asked as I pulled to a stop at the top of my driveway.

Without answering him, I hopped out of the truck and retrieved the money from its hiding place. I counted it out and was glad to see it was all there. I stuffed it back into the tin box and tucked it beneath the seat once I climbed behind the wheel again. "Where should we go?" I asked.

"Aren't we already here?" He looked around. "This is your place, right?"

"We don't have to go in there. We can—"

He gripped my hand. "Yes, we do. You saved me from my hell, and it's time for me to repay the favor. I won't let anything happen to you. Go to the house."

He didn't leave any room for argument. I put the truck in drive, and it rattled as we rumbled over the driveway full of potholes I never knew how to fix. There were a lot of things I didn't know how to fix, but I thought I could maybe try to fix Alex. I had no clue what I was doing with my captor. Bringing him into my home—a place that didn't feel any safer than his.

As the house came into view, my mouth went dry. What the hell would I say to my father? How could I explain where I'd been and why I'd brought a stranger into his sanctuary? The place that had been hell for most of my life. The place that haunted and hurt me in different ways.

I turned off the ignition, and the ancient engine sputtered to a stop, leaving us in silence. Alex's eyes trailed over the property with a boyish curiosity that almost made me smile. I wasn't sure what he was gawking at, though. There was nothing special about my old house. The crumbling concrete and mismatched siding showcased its age and condition. The grass hadn't been cut since I'd been gone, and the summer sunshine had fed it well. His house hadn't been much better, but I still found a flush of embarrassment creeping into my cheeks.

"What about your father?" he asked.

I swallowed hard. I wasn't sure what we'd walk into. It scared the hell out of me, but I had no choice. I had to be strong.

"Stay here," I said, though I wasn't sure why. Maybe it was to keep him from seeing how we lived. The graveyard of bottles. The corpses of dirty dishes and half-eaten meals that likely littered the counters. More embarrassment. Or maybe I thought it would be easier to speak to my father without Alex by my side. Either way, I felt it was something I had to do alone.

I took another step, but his hand clamped around my wrist.

"There's no way in hell I'm letting you go in there by yourself," he said, his voice firm and unwavering.

Again, he left no room for argument, so we got out of the truck, setting foot into purgatory the moment we stepped into the knee-high grass. The steps creaked with my meager weight as I placed my feet on them, and my hand lingered on the rusty metal doorknob as I worried about all the skeletons tumbling into the daylight once I opened that door. It wasn't just a closet full of them. They filled the house.

When I walked inside, the dusty smell of age welcomed me home. It was a scent that had been a staple my entire life, and it was all I'd known before Alex and his brother gave me something to compare it to. I hated the smell I bathed in at their house, but I couldn't decide which was worse: dust and mold or sweat and death.

Shame gripped me again as we entered the hall and I looked around. Through the kitchen doorway I could see the flies circling the moldy food residue on the plates scattered across the countertops. Empty bottles dotted the table in the hall. They hadn't been there when I left, which meant he'd managed to get more alcohol somehow. I wrapped my arms around myself and glared at the staircase my father often drunkenly climbed to get to me. I shivered at the memories.

Warm arms wrapped around me, and I jumped and turned around, trying to stop the panicked spasm in my throat, trying to slow my galloping heart before it broke through my sternum and landed on the floor.

"What's the matter?" Alex whispered, wiping the sweat

that had gathered at my temples. "I've done some pretty shitty things to you, and you didn't react that violently. I didn't understand just how bad it was, but I think I'm beginning to." He set his jaw and looked toward the living room. I recognized that fiery look in his eyes. Someone was about to pay for their mistakes, and this time it wouldn't be me.

Chapter Twenty-Two

Alexzander

The girl in front of me wasn't the same girl I'd seen in my house. Not even at her weakest was she as shook up as she was in that moment. Was it worse than what Gunnir had put her through? Or was it worse because the assault came from someone related to her? Family never felt like family in our home. It just meant we shared the same blood, and as The Man used to always say, *come is thicker than blood*.

"Is he in the living room?" I asked.

She closed her eyes, and a tear shimmied down her cheek and leapt from her jaw. I'd seen enough. I took a few steps around the corner and wondered if she found it odd that I knew the layout of her house. If she realized I'd stalked her long before I took her. I'd soon be out of her life forever, so it didn't matter.

But first, I had to make sure she was safe.

The back of the chair faced me, and a half-empty bottle of rum stood beside it. A man's head peeked just above the back of the chair, his attention focused on a grainy program flickering across a television's dusty screen. Every now and again he'd reach down, gulp a swig of liquor, and put the bottle back in its place. Had he noticed she was gone? Did he even fucking care? What kind of father continued to drink himself into oblivion while his daughter was missing? My father did a lot of terrible shit, but he never forgot about me. But my father also didn't sexually assault me. Not directly, at least.

I shuffled forward a step, and the floor groaned beneath me.

"Baby girl? Is that you?" his deep, watery voice called out. The way he said the pet name made my body react in ways I'd never felt. "Grab me a beer from the fridge and come sit on my lap." He spoke in a tone that no father should use toward their kin. His creepy voice crawled through my veins like sludge, and I could only imagine how it affected Ophelia. I looked back at her. Her legs pressed together, and I knew what was happening to her body. I knew what happened when genuine, deeply ingrained, mind-altering fear squeezes your insides and fills you with the urge to piss. When you can't even see what's in front of you or draw a breath because you're in a blind panic. I knew that look on her face and the tremble in her limbs and the way she clenched her knees together, because I had felt that kind of fear myself.

It broke me to see her experiencing it. Ophelia's reaction to the mere sound of her father's voice made me fucking homicidal. Made me rabid for her revenge.

I reached behind me and pulled my hunting knife from the holder on my belt. I took a step forward, but a hand on my shoulder stopped me.

"Alex . . ." she whispered with a weak shake of her head. Her father didn't even hear her over the sound of the TV show and the deafening effect of alcohol.

I guided her backward until her spine met with the wall.

"Don't try to stop me. He deserves to rot in hell with *my* father."

Her eyes searched mine, and the trembling stilled. "Why would you be the one to do it? I'm the one he's touched."

I smirked at her words and leaned in to plant a kiss on the mouth that spoke them. Atta girl. She was speaking a language I could understand. I had been the one to take my father's life because I harbored the most hurt. I had poisoned him and watched life leave his eyes with the marks from a whipping still fresh and oozing on my back. Everyone has a limit, and he'd reached mine. Her father surpassed hers the first time he touched her. Even so, I wasn't willing to put her in harm's way. I only had the one knife. If he disarmed her, I had no way of effectively protecting her.

"I won't risk him hurting you more than he already has," I said. Her eyes pleaded with me to hand her the knife, but she didn't argue with words.

With the confidence of a man who *has* killed before, I marched toward the chair in the living room. "Hello, father of the year," I said, circling into his view.

He looked pathetic. A puddle of vomit had dried on his ripped undershirt, and the flannel over it hung off his too-slim frame. He probably hadn't eaten much since Ophelia left. Well . . . since she was taken. He wiped crumbs off his beard and tried to stand, but he flopped back twice before finally finding his feet. It almost seemed unfair to attack a man so helplessly drunk. Then again, he'd had no problems attacking a helpless child, so that evened things out a bit.

"Who the fuck are you?" he snarled. A vapor cloud of old liquor crashed into my face. He smelled like a fermented batch of whiskey in a brewery, and it was nearly enough to make me cough.

I felt Ophelia's presence behind me, so I reached back and pulled her to my side. She kept her eyes pinned to the ground in front of us, focused on the bourbon bottle. "You don't need to know who I am, but you know who this is, right?"

He coughed. "Yeah, that's my little girl."

"You don't have the right to call her that. If she was your little girl, you shouldn't have touched—"

"I don't touch my daughter!" he yelled, stumbling forward a step.

Ophelia's eyes shot up to him, and a bolt of anger rushed onto her face and twisted her beautiful features into something sinister. "Yes you do!" she said. "How dare you deny it! How dare you—" Her chest hitched and cut off her sentence.

"If I ever touched you wrong, it's because I mistook you for your mother," he said, and it was the lamest fucking excuse I'd ever heard. "It's not my fault."

Her lower jaw quivered, but she found her voice. "When I was eight, Dad?"

"Don't fucking call him that," I said. "The men who contributed to our DNA don't have the privilege of being called Dad because they never earned it. They were never fathers. That's why I called mine The Man. Call yours whatever you'd like. Shit bag. Sperm donor. Filthy goddamn pedo. Call him whatever you want, but do not call him Dad."

Her father's attention jumped to me. "She's lying to you. She's an attention-seeking brat. She always has been."

If he thought I would turn on Ophelia over some haggard drunk's words, he had a nice surprise coming to him. Something really humbling.

Rage flashed across his face when I didn't buy the bullshit he'd tried to shovel down my throat. He took a step toward Ophelia, but I got between them and lifted my knife into view. "What are you gonna do, punk? Stab me?"

"That's exactly what I'm going to do, you sick fuck." I thrust the knife into his gut, and he fell into me. Blood crept from a darkening spot in his undershirt and slid around my hand. I ripped the knife backward and pushed him off me. He fell onto his recliner with a heavy thud, and even mortally wounded, he reached for his bottle. I steadied my grip on the knife, assuming he'd try to use the bottle as a weapon, but he only twisted off the cap and tilted the bottle's mouth toward his lips. "What the fuck is wrong with you, old man?"

"There ain't nothing right about me," he wheezed. "Better make amends with the lord now, I guess."

"The lord doesn't want your amends," I said as I handed the knife to Ophelia. She looked at me for permission as she wrapped her fingers around the handle. She didn't need permission to get the vengeance she deserved, and now that he was too weak to fight back, she could safely get it.

She stepped toward him and leaned forward, the knife at her side. "Admit you touched me."

"I'm not admitting shit," he snarled back, a trail of blood falling from the side of his mouth as he talked.

"Admit it!" she screamed, tears strangling her words.

I grabbed her shoulder. "There are two types of evil men in this world. One brags about what they've done, and one denies it." I wasn't sure which was scarier or more sinister. Her father or mine. Two people who destroyed their family and built a world around them that fueled only pain. My father was fucking evil. This man was evil in a different way. Regardless, the devil would fuck both their asses equally for all of eternity. "This man is a pussy, O. He'll never admit what he's done to you. If you want your vengeance, take it now, before it's too late. My father yelled his evils from the rooftops, but yours will take his vile secret to the grave. Saying it out loud means acknowledging his sick lust for children. His *own* fucking child. Admitting it means it wasn't some drunk stupor he made up to rationalize what he'd done." I turned my attention to him. "There's not enough alcohol in the world to drink away those desires, you sick fuck." I promised her vengeance, but I couldn't help taking a swing at him. I hauled my fist forward, knocking his head into the headrest.

Ophelia followed my jab by stabbing the knife into his chest. She ripped it out and plunged it in again. His eyes widened in a look of shocked betrayal. He'd never expected her to fight back, but she was stronger than he'd realized. Stronger than I'd realized.

Ophelia released the knife's handle and turned toward me. Blood mixed with the tears on her face and ran in faded rivers toward her jaw. Her chest heaved and I knew she needed comfort, but I had no idea how to comfort another person. Even with my mother, the best I could do was to make sure she knew she wasn't alone. I was just present. I knew how to do that. I sure as hell wasn't the empathetic person she probably needed right then.

I put my arms around her and held her awkwardly, and she started sobbing, her whole body lurching from the power behind her pain. Her knees gave way, and I caught her and lowered her to the ground. She curled up on herself, and I sat behind her and rubbed her back as her heaving sobs turned into numb and broken whimpers. She needed more, and I wanted to give her more, but I just didn't know how to help someone who was this upset.

I laid her on her back and climbed over her, pinning her with some of my weight until her heaving chest slowed beneath me. She dug her nails into my outstretched arms, and I just made myself present. I was just a thing she could dig and claw into as she fought off the man who would always haunt her. Her hands left my arms and pressed against my chest. A guttural scream left her mouth as she balled up her hands and sent weak punches into my sides.

"Fuck you!" she yelled as her hands fell to the wooden floor. She'd run out of fight in front of my eyes. She landed a

final kick that knocked the bourbon bottle onto its side, and the smell wrapped around us.

"Get it out," I told her.

"That fuck you wasn't toward you," she said with a deflated breath.

I smirked. "Some of it might have been." We stared at each other as the silence hung between us. "Sorry I don't know how to do this better. I'm not used to dealing with trauma I didn't cause." I released her and she sat up beside me.

"What did we do?" she asked, her shoulders finally relaxing.

"This was nothing. At least *he* deserved it."

"Even if he deserved it, we just took a life. I don't even know how to cover up something like this." She gestured toward her father's body.

"I'll handle that part. I'll wrap him in something, toss him in the back of the truck, and drop him into the pit with all the other demons. Does he have any friends? Anyone that might come looking for him?"

She shook her head. "I usually buy everything he needs. He just sits in that chair and drinks himself stupid. He rarely leaves the house."

"That's convenient for you, then. Just keep shopping as if you're buying for two people."

Her gaze snapped to me. "I *will* be buying for two people. You'll be here."

"I can't stay here, O. I've made sure you'll be safe, and I'll stick around long enough to help out around here for a bit, but then I need to move on. I don't know how to live a normal life, and I can't guarantee I won't hurt you again. I don't know how to be a human being."

"How can you say you don't know how to be a human being?" she said as I pulled away from her.

"Because I wasn't raised like a human being." I was mildly annoyed with her statement. How human had I been to her?

"You want affection, you feel bad when you see someone hurting, and you want to love. You're human."

"I want *your* affection. I feel bad when *you* hurt. I've never felt this way about anyone else. I've felt some levels of bad when horrible things happened to girls because of me or Gunnir, but with you, it makes my heart actually feel heavy. Like, real low in my chest." I held my hand level with my chest and pushed it down. "I'm only human for you, O."

"If you aren't human, what do you see yourself as?"

"The devil," I said, much too sure of my words.

She dropped her gaze. "Well, I don't feel too human either. I'm just a ghost hanging around the empty shell of what I was." She raised her eyes to mine. "But you make me feel alive. Even in the worst moments with you, I was glad I could finally feel something again." Her cheeks flushed and I worried she would cry again. I leaned into her and kissed her, drawing away enough to touch my forehead to hers.

"Then I guess we can be inhuman together. For a little while, at least."

CHAPTER TWENTY-THREE

OPHELIA

I awoke the next morning in my bed. Alex insisted on sleeping on the couch, and half of me wondered if he did that to prevent me from leaving in the middle of the night. I never considered that maybe he planned to escape while I slept. I shook off that fear when I heard the lawnmower rumbling to life below my bedroom window. When I peeled back the tattered curtains, I saw Alex in the backyard. He wiped sweat from his forehead as he leaned back, baring his shirtless chest to the sun. His skin glistened with perspiration. Even as my mouth watered for him, I could never forget the things he'd done to me.

But I also couldn't forget the things he'd done *for* me. He had a hold on me.

I got out of bed and slipped a robe over my cami and pajama pants. It felt so good to be in my own clothes again. I walked downstairs and made coffee like I hadn't been ripped from my routine and held captive until just the night before. I watched through the kitchen window as Alex tried to tame the jungle sprawling across our yard. He dug his heels into the earth and pushed the mower through the overgrown grass. His body flexed with the exertion, and I felt the need to hold my jaw in place so it wouldn't fall to the floor. *He probably got ripped like that from hauling dead bodies,* I thought, and it sent a shiver up my spine.

Alex snatched his undershirt from his pocket and wiped at his forehead. He turned off the mower and came inside. "Hey," he said as the door closed behind him. "You're gonna need a helluva lot more gas to tackle that lawn." He wiped his forehead again and sat down at the kitchen table. I grabbed a couple of mugs from the cabinet and poured fresh coffee into them. He liked it black. I preferred it with milk and sugar, but the milk had spoiled in my absence, so I did the best I could with the sugar. I set the cup in front of him, and he leaned over and inhaled the aroma. "Thanks."

I sat across from him and sipped my coffee. The sugar didn't cut the bitter taste, but I needed the caffeine. "Did you . . . take care of my father?"

He nodded and picked at the side of his thumb. "I handled it before the sun came up. Dropped by the neighbors' houses to cover our tracks too. They bought it."

We sat in silence for a moment.

"This is weird, Alex," I said into my mug.

"What is?"

"Us being together in my house. Talking about disposing of dead bodies and explaining to the neighbors why you burned the house down. Fucking weird."

"I figured it would be too much for you. I'll do what I can for some of the shit that's broken around here, then I'll leave you to it. You don't owe me anything, but if you can at least give me a head start before you call the cops, I'd appreciate it." He rose from the table and went outside before I could formulate a response.

Well, that escalated faster than I expected. I never even got the chance to explain what I was thinking. He just vomited his plan and left. What about my plan? What about what I wanted?

I ripped open the door and pushed my bare feet through the mangled grass until I found him bent over and tinkering with a pipe attached to the side of the house.

"You aren't leaving me here like this," I said, as firmly as I could muster.

"Like what?" he asked.

I struggled to find the words that would describe how I felt. "When I said things were weird, I didn't just mean the weird shit we've been through. I also mean these feelings I have that I can't rationalize."

He rose to his feet and walked toward me and stood close enough that I could feel the heat from his sun-warmed body. "What the hell are you saying?"

"I'm saying that despite everything, I fell for you, Alex. If I can push through my fear, so can you. Stop being afraid. Stop trying to run."

"How the hell could you fall for someone like me? It was easy for me to fall for you, but I hurt you. I really hurt you." He looked into my eyes and softened his voice. "Love has never been kind to you, has it, Ophelia?"

I shook my head, tears welling in my eyes and blurring his face.

"Love has always hurt you, huh?"

I nodded.

"Then why would you still chase after it? Why would you still want what hurts you?"

"If you want to leave because you can't see a life with me, I won't hold you back, but if you plan to leave because you can see a life with me, you're nothing but a coward. You're so focused on the pain you caused me, but you forget about all you've done for me. You fought so hard to keep me safe from Gunnir. To keep me alive. You killed your own brother to stop his assault. You killed my father to make sure he couldn't hurt me anymore. If you leave, you'll kill me too."

My words struck him in the face, and I was glad. I wouldn't let him pretend that leaving meant keeping me safe. He needed to know the truth. He didn't get to walk away because things were complicated and confusing. I wouldn't let him. Even as his fists balled at his sides and the frustration brewed behind his eyes, I wouldn't let him give up on this. Or himself.

ALEXZANDER

I WALKED toward the front of the house and shivered as her words reeled through my mind. I killed my brother. I killed The Man. I killed her father. It was my hand that destroyed the monsters that lurked in the shadows. I even tried to kill the last monster, but the little lamb had dragged the big bad wolf from the burning building.

She followed me, cornering me just inside the front door.

I turned and gripped her shoulders. "What about all the things I did *to* you? How can you act like I didn't put you through hell?"

A tear ran down her cheek and dripped onto my hand. "Please don't ask me to explain why and how I've forgiven all you've done. I don't have the answers!"

She shrugged off my hands and stepped into me, only to lay blows to my chest. It hurt, but I deserved to feel some of her pain. All of it, actually. But no matter how much her anger fueled her, she could never hurt me in the ways I'd hurt her.

"Fuck you for being the source of my pain *and* my comfort!" she shouted. "Fuck you for becoming a friend instead of an enemy! I hate you for not killing your brother sooner. I hate that you're willing to leave me! Fuck you!"

"Please—"

"No! I'm not done." She let out a primal scream and thrust her fist into my gut, forcing the air from my lungs.

I bent over to catch my breath. Anger tightened my skin, but I wouldn't hurt Ophelia for hitting me. She'd figure shit out. She was stronger than anyone I knew, including myself.

She inhaled a sharp breath. "I hate you for making me fall for you. I hate that the thought of a life without you makes me fucking sick, because it should be the opposite. I should be glad you want to leave!" She stopped to catch her breath, and I didn't interrupt her tirade. I wanted her to get it all out, no matter how much the words hurt. "If you walk out that door, you're taking the only part of me that feels something. Haven't you taken enough from me?"

She tried to look away, but I gripped her chin and forced her to look at me. "Do you really think I want to leave? I don't, but you're better off without me and the painful memories between us. I want you to stay mine so fucking bad. I'm absolutely rabid for that. I'm ready to let you go because it means freeing you from all the hurt I caused you. But for some fucked-up reason, you want to stay mine."

Her lower lip quivered above my hand. She needed to understand what she was asking.

I took a step forward, forcing her backward until she met the wall. "Be careful what you ask for, O. Are you sure you want me to stay? If you say no, I'll get out of your life forever. You'll never have to worry about me waiting in the shadows. But if you say yes, you're saying yes to all that I am."

"I'm saying yes," she whispered.

My hand rose to her throat, and a whimper squeezed past

her lips. I inhaled that sound, breathing it into my lungs. It felt so familiar and wrong, but I was still like Pavlov's dogs. I was still conditioned to salivate any time I heard it. "That sound still goes right to my dick," I growled against her lips. "Does that scare you?"

She shook her head. "Not anymore."

"You should always be a little afraid of me. I'm a Bruggar, after all."

She looked into my eyes, and I didn't see fear there anymore. I saw desire and need. I never thought she'd want to be with me once she got a taste of freedom again. A beautiful girl like her could have gotten anyone she wanted, but she was choosing the demon that lurked in her nightmares. The demon who *became* her nightmare. She somehow threw a cape on me in her mind and thought I had saved her from the horror I put her in.

My heart hammered against my chest, unable to comprehend what was happening.

"I know it's hard to understand," she said, "and I won't pretend you didn't break me, but you're also the one who put me back together again. Now you're the glue holding all those pieces in place."

I smirked at her words. "That's crazy to me because you broke me as well. Ripped me apart and let the light shine through the cracks. You didn't just put me back together, though. You rearranged everything before you did."

"That's why I'm not scared of you. Even if you take me like you used to, it wouldn't hurt like it once did."

My hand dropped from her throat and landed on her chest above her breasts. I felt the beat of her heart beneath my fingertips, calm and even. I breathed in her scent. "Remember when I made you come?" I whispered in her ear.

She nodded.

"I loved how you fought the pleasure until you couldn't

anymore, and I realized how much I liked making you feel good. I liked what your pleasure did to me. How it humanized me." I brushed the hair from her forehead. "I don't know how to be what you need me to be, but I'm willing to try if you'll promise me something."

"What?" she asked.

"If I fail at this, if I fail to be good to you, you'll make me leave, okay?" I rested a hot hand on her cheek. "Promise me you'll make me leave."

"I promise," she whispered.

"This doesn't mean I'll fuck you gently. I'm still me. I'm still selfish, especially when it comes to your body. But if you say no, Ophelia, I'll try my damnedest to stop for you." I bit her lower lip as I lowered the front of her cami and gripped her breast. She moaned into my mouth, and the sound made me throb. I tugged down her shorts and kissed her as I freed my dick. I'd never wanted to be inside her more. Never wanted to feel heaven so badly.

"Alex," she whispered as my lips brushed against her neck.

I lifted her thigh, haunted for a moment as I remembered the last time I'd fucked her like this and how much horror had come after the pleasure. We both had memories that would plague us forever. We'd also found an escape from our torment.

With each other.

"I love you, Ophelia, and I refuse to let love hurt you this time."

She wrapped her arms around me and dug her nails into my back as I fucked her. "I love you, Alex," she whispered in my ear.

I stopped and looked into her eyes. "Tell me again."

"I love you."

I wrapped my hand around the back of her neck and pushed inside her until I met her end. It wasn't enough. I couldn't get deep enough. I dragged her to the kitchen and bent her over the table, gripping her hips to give me more control over her perfect body. I leaned my weight over her and pushed within her, thrusting as deep as I could. She whimpered as I took her in such a familiar yet foreign way. Familiar because it was her but foreign because everything was free. Her decision to fuck me. My decision to stay. It was the first time I'd had a choice, and I knew it was the same for her. Somehow, she'd found freedom within captivity, but I found mine within her.

Epilogue
One Month Later

Alexzander

Freedom was hard for me at first. Simple things like having coffee in the morning or waking up beside an unchained woman made me anxious. It felt strange. It felt wrong. I didn't know what to do with myself when I had the choice to do anything. Ophelia helped as much as she could, though, and I was learning how to live.

"Hey," she said as she came into the living room and sat in the chair across from me, a wooden coffee table between us. "You okay?"

I nodded, but I couldn't fool her. Some days were harder than others.

"I have something that might cheer you up," she said with a smile. She reached beneath the table and brought out a box I recognized immediately—tattered cardboard with a graphic across the top that had faded with age. She opened it and laid out the board and the pieces. She'd run a thin strip of silver duct tape down the center of the board and used Sharpies to fill in the squares. It had been messed up for years, and now it was whole again. Ophelia was good at putting broken things back together.

We could have afforded a new board—she'd taken a different job with better pay closer to the city, and I did odd jobs for local farmers—but we liked this little piece of our past. Not all memories hurt.

Once she set it up, she looked at me with a sinful bite of her lips. "Ready to play?" she asked, and my eyes leapt from her perfect mouth to the checkers game between us.

"You know I'll end up fucking you before you even get to my king's row, right?"

"We shall see," she said as she leaned over to make her first move.

I made a return move and stared at her. This game was the one thing I could bring from my old life into our new one. One thing that felt normal in a world of unusual. It felt safe.

"Are you cornered, O?" I asked after a few more moves. It wasn't often that I got the upper hand, but sometimes I did.

She bit her lip in that way that drove me mad, and I adjusted my pants as she expertly maneuvered herself to a better position. She got out of the predicament I put her in and ended up taking over the game.

When she'd thoroughly beaten me, I could only look across the table and smile. "There's only one other person I have ever loved, and that was my mother. You remind me so much of her." As soon as it came out of my mouth, I realized how odd it sounded. But it was true.

"That's a really fucking weird thing to say, Alex," she said with a laugh.

A smirk crossed my lips. "Don't make it weirder than it is. You're just strong like she was. My mother reminded me that I had a heart, every day. You were the only other person to see what was inside me." I leaned forward, closed the distance between us, and kissed her. "I love you, Ophelia," I whispered against her lips.

OPHELIA

HEARING him say he loved me made my heart beat harder against my chest. Everyone that ever claimed to love me had hurt me. Even Alex. Somehow, as he snaked his hand around the back of my neck and drew me in for another kiss, I believed this love would be different. The gentle way his fingers brushed the back of my neck made me forget about the rough touches. But sometimes I found myself yearning for those rough touches. I'd never understand how his brain worked, but that was okay because I didn't understand mine either. I'd fallen in love with the man of my nightmares, and it didn't have to make sense.

I gripped the hem of my shirt and pulled it over my head.

"Ophelia," he warned, but he didn't need to.

I knew what he would do, and I welcomed it.

His eyes remained locked on me as I lowered my pajama pants and kicked them away. He rose from the chair, pushed the coffee table out of the way, and stood in front of me as he removed his sweatpants. He put his hands to either side of my chair, bracketing me between his powerful arms, and he kissed me. Hard and driven and full of need. He lifted me as if I weighed nothing at all and pinned me against the wall. I wrapped my legs around him, and the hard warmth of his cock rested between us. He drew his hips back and put himself inside me, and I dropped my head against the wall as he filled me. A growl rose from his throat and vibrated against my lips.

"My god, O, you feel incredible." His mouth lowered to

my neck, and he nipped my skin. "When everything was wrong, you were so damn right."

"Lay me down and fuck me like you still have me under lock and key," I whispered before kissing his mouth.

He carried me to the throw rug covering the old hardwood floors and placed me on my back. He dropped to his knees, hooked his hands around my thighs, and tugged me closer to him. There was a moment of panic when I remembered a time not so long ago when I turned over and saw him between my legs. It was eerily similar, but there was a difference this time.

I wanted him.

He leaned over me and kissed my breasts. "I won't fuck you like a captive, O, but I'll fuck you like I still own you, because your body is mine. This is mine," he whispered as he kissed the skin above my heart. "And this too." He lifted his head and bypassed my lips to kiss my forehead.

Alex curled his hips forward and pushed inside me. I dropped my head back and let the tears slip past the crease of my eyelids as he fucked me. I couldn't help it. I felt an overwhelming rush of intense love for the first time in my entire life, and it came from the last person I expected. My tears were laced with a happiness I had never experienced. Alex knew my pain, and I knew his. I felt it in every thrust as he tried to help us forget all the hurt we experienced. He made love to me like I was a reflection of himself, and for once, he liked what he saw staring back at him.

He sat up and grazed my slit with his fingers. He fucked me like his life depended on my pleasure, and I would happily give it to him. His thumb stroked my clit and my nails dug into his sides as he brought me closer and closer.

I drew him into me and panted against his shoulder as he rubbed me until I was so close. So damn close.

"I can feel you tightening, O. Stop thinking about it. Stop

trying to come and just let it happen," he whispered as he moved his thumb along my clit.

I focused on the way his cock stretched me and how his fingers felt as he stroked me. His weight pressed into me with each powerful thrust, sinking into my—

He growled as I shuddered and clenched around him. "That's a good fucking girl," he whispered. His hips stuttered against mine as he rode out my orgasm. "And you're mine," he growled as he came inside me, chasing my come with his. He leaned down and kissed me.

Alexzander emerged from the depths of hell and shielded me from the devil as he raised us until we felt the first cool breeze hit our faces. He tried to leave me at the gates, but I wouldn't let him. He earned his way back up here, on earth, by my side. People will wonder how I could lie with a demon, but demons are only fallen angels, and Alex fell pretty fucking hard. He was just willing to stand up again and live up to his name.

If you like dark and depraved stories like this one, check out *Never Let Go*, another dark captive/captors horror romance. Books2read.com/NLG

If you like your depraved stories with a little more spice, check out *Toxic Love* and *Toxic Desires*. This story was once banned for content and is not for the faint of heart either! Start here: Books2read.com/Toxic-Love

Both books are also available in audio format with duet narration

CONNECT WITH LAUREN

Check out LaurenBiel.com to sign up for the newsletter and get VIP (free and first) access to Lauren's spicy novellas and other bonus content!

Join the group on Facebook to connect with other fans and to discuss the books with the author. Visit http://www.facebook.com/groups/laurenbieltraumances for more!

Lauren is now on Patreon! Get access to even more content and sneak peeks at upcoming novels. Check it out at www.patreon.com/LaurenBielAuthor to learn more!

Acknowledgments

I would like to extend a big un-thank you to my husband, who gave several unfortunate ideas, like the jar and the soda bottle. He continues to support me as my author journey gets darker. He's my biggest fan, and I'm so thankful!

This story would never have come together as well as it did without my incredible friend/editor Brooke! If you asked me if I'd ever make her edit a book as depraved as this one, I'd have told you . . . yeah, probably! Thank you for being open-minded and for remaining my friend when I'm an author-zilla.

Thank you to my PA, Christina Santos, for the unending support.

A lot of my betas backed out of this one. For those who stuck around and read this, I love you—in a weird way. Danielle G., Ash, Jay, Kolleen, Christina, Reneé, Nuzhat, and others!

I wouldn't be able to do this without these special patrons: Lori (Special love your way, friend!), Nineette, Rachel, Amy W., Ariel, Kimberly B., Jay, Jessica, Dimitra, Venetta, and @doseofdarkromance.

ALSO BY LAUREN BIEL

To view Lauren Biel's complete list of books, visit: https://www.
amazon.com/Lauren-Biel/e/B09CQYDK87

ABOUT THE AUTHOR

Lauren Biel is the author of many dark romance books with several more titles in the works. When she's not working, she's writing. When she's not writing, she's spending time with her husband, her friends, or her pets. You might also find her on a horseback trail ride or sitting beside a waterfall in Upstate New York. When reading her work, expect the unexpected.

To be the first to know about her upcoming titles, please visit www.LaurenBiel.com.